HOW TO CATCH A
POLAR BEAR

STACY DeKEYSER

HOW TO CATCH A POLAR BEAR

MARGARET K. McELDERRY BOOKS
NEW YORK   LONDON   TORONTO   SYDNEY   NEW DELHI

MARGARET K. McELDERRY BOOKS

An imprint of Simon & Schuster Children's Publishing Division

1230 Avenue of the Americas, New York, New York 10020

This book is a work of fiction. Any references to historical events, real people, or real places are used fictitiously. Other names, characters, places, and events are products of the author's imagination, and any resemblance to actual events or places or persons, living or dead, is entirely coincidental.

MARGARET K. McELDERRY BOOKS is a trademark of Simon & Schuster, Inc.

For information about special discounts for bulk purchases, please contact Simon & Schuster Special Sales at 1-866-506-1949 or business@simonandschuster.com.

The Simon & Schuster Speakers Bureau can bring authors to your live event. For more information or to book an event, contact the Simon & Schuster Speakers Bureau at 1-866-248-3049 or visit our website at www.simonspeakers.com.

Interior design by Irene Metaxatos

The text for this book was set in Palatino LT Std.

Manufactured in the United States of America

0523 FFG

First Edition

10 9 8 7 6 5 4 3 2 1

CIP data for this book is available from the Library of Congress.

ISBN 9781665925617

ISBN 9781665925631(ebook)

FOR NICKI

Κούκλα μου

CHAPTER

1

THE SUMMER OF 1948 STARTED WITH A BANG.

Or, I should say, a crash.

It was early morning on the first day of summer vacation, and I was still half asleep. If you're a delicate sort of person, skip the rest of this sentence, because I was lying on top of the sheets in my underwear. Sorry about that, but it was the middle of a heat wave. My bedroom window was wide open, but that didn't help. I couldn't feel even the hint of a breeze.

I tried to distract myself by imagining everything that would make this the best summer ever. No more sixth grade. Swimming at the lakefront. Ball games at Orchard Field.

CRASH!

I opened my eyes. Someone—or something—was out in the alley behind the house. Raccoons in the garbage cans again? Or maybe Ace's little sister left her roller skates out (again), and the milkman tripped over them (again). Whatever it was, I was too sleepy and too sticky to get up and look.

Downstairs in the kitchen, the radio hummed to life. Ma was up early, as usual. Maybe she had taken the garbage out and had knocked over the trash cans by accident.

Top o' the morning, folks! It's your ol' pals Ray and Bob here on WTRJ radio, helping you start your day.

BOB: It's gonna be another hot one, folks. The mercury will be working its way up to ninety-one degrees today.

RAY: It might be a good day to head on down to the lakefront, don't you think, Bob?

BOB: Or you could go to a nice air-conditioned movie theater. Sit back and enjoy that new John Wayne picture in cool comfort.

CRASH!
Now I sat up in bed.

That wasn't Ma. I could hear her rattling around in the kitchen downstairs.

I hopped out of bed and poked my head out the window. "Holy smokes!"

I blinked. I rubbed my eyes and looked again.

Something had knocked over the trash cans, all right.

But it wasn't a raccoon, and it wasn't the milkman tripping over roller skates.

It was a polar bear.

CHAPTER

2

I BET YOU'RE THINKING THAT I'M MAKING THIS UP, OR that maybe I was still dreaming. But what if I told you that we live three blocks from the city zoo? Where a polar bear also lives?

I looked out the window again. Now it was wandering up the alley, checking out the neighbors' garbage cans.

CRASH!

In the distance, I heard sirens. They got louder and louder, and then they stopped.

I got dressed as quick as I could and raced down the stairs.

"Polar bear!" I gasped, busting into the kitchen.

Ma glanced up from the stove. "Nicky! You are up early.

Have some eggs." She set a plate in front of Pop, who was already at the table, reading the morning paper.

"But, Ma!" I pointed toward the back door, which was wide open, leaving nothing but an old screen door between us and an actual polar bear. "Didn't you hear the sirens? There's a wild animal out there!" I hurried across the room and slammed the door shut.

"It's too hot!" said Ma. She stomped over and opened the door again.

Uncle Spiro came rattling down the stairs, dressed for work in his white shirt and bow tie. His soda-jerk hat was folded flat and tucked into his shirtfront pocket. "What's this about wild animals?"

"In the alley!" I told him. "A polar bear!"

"Very funny, Nick," he said, pulling up a chair. "Athena, have you seen my clean apron?"

"On the wash line," said Ma, waving toward the backyard. "Nicky, go get Spiro's apron for him, *neh?*"

"But, Ma!"

We interrupt this program to bring you a special bulletin.

RAY: Shortly after five o'clock this morning, a full-grown polar bear was reported missing from the city zoo.

"I told you!"

"I thought you were joking!" said Uncle Spiro.

"How can someone lose a polar bear?" said Pop.

"Shut the door!" hollered Ma.

RAY: The half-ton critter—

BOB: It says here his name is Frosty.

RAY: —was spotted an hour later by one Clement Baratka, a local milkman, who reported that the bear knocked over a backyard fence and spilled trash cans.

BOB: I'll bet that milkman spilled a gallon or two, if you know what I mean.

"*Our* trash cans!" I blurted, pointing toward the back alley. "I saw it with my own eyes!"

"I hope that was not *our* milkman," said Pop, turning a page of his newspaper. "I am not paying for spilled milk."

RAY: Hang on, folks, we have an update. We're being told that the bear was apprehended by police officers without incident and is being returned to the zoo as we speak.

BOB: Without incident? What about poor ol' Clem? He almost got his butter churned!

RAY: This is no time for jokes, Bob.

BOB: Who's joking? Say, don't you wish you could've seen our brave men in blue stuffing ol' Frosty into the back seat of their squad car?

RAY: I don't think that's how it happened, Bob.

BOB: Then answer me one question, Ray.

RAY: What's that?

BOB: How *do* you catch a polar bear?

This concludes our special report. We now return you to our regularly scheduled program.

Ma snapped off the radio and glared at it like it had personally insulted her. "Now we have to move!"

Pop looked up from his newspaper. "Move? Why? More coffee, please."

Ma sloshed coffee into Pop's mug and clanked the pot back onto the stove. "It's too dangerous, living only three blocks from that zoo. A polar bear, it almost walked right into our house! Spiro, you'd better go. What if he broke into your shop?"

Uncle Spiro chuckled. "I don't think polar bears eat frozen custard, but it's time for me to head down there anyway." He gulped his coffee, grabbed the car keys off their hook by the back door, and left.

"I can't believe I saw a real polar bear," I said. "In *our* alley! I gotta go tell Ace!"

"Don't go outside, Nicky!" said Ma.

"But, Ma, you heard the radio," I told her. "The coast is clear. Besides, I've lived here for twelve whole years so far, and it's the first time I've ever seen a wild animal out back." Which was kind of disappointing, now that I thought about it.

The back door swung open and hit the wall with a bang. There was Ace, still in his pajamas. "Nick! Did ya hear?"

"Close the door!" hollered Ma. "Wild animals!"

"Ace! *Kalimera*," said Pop, which means "good morning." My folks were born in Greece, so a lot of what they say is in Greek. I don't think they even realize it.

"I saw it!" I told Ace. "With my own eyes!"

"No kidding?" said Ace. "Jeepers! You have all the luck! Something sure smells good."

Ma cracked an egg into the pan. "Fried or scrambled?"

"Fried, please," said Ace, pulling up a chair. "Over easy."

Ace is my best pal. He lives next door. He likes to think he also lives with us, especially when something's cooking.

"What kind of world we are living in?" muttered Ma,

cracking more eggs. "Dangerous animals escaping all the time." She turned and shook her spatula at me. "Nicky, you stay in the house this summer."

Pop folded his newspaper. "Athena, you worry too much. These things, they don't happen *all the time*."

"Oh no?" said Ma, plopping plates of eggs in front of me and Ace. "What about 1929?"

Pop frowned for a second, and then his bushy eyebrows shot up from behind his glasses. "Oh, that? It was only a monkey."

"A monkey got out?" said Ace. "What happened?"

"I'll tell you what happened," said Ma. "A monkey. It got out!"

"Holy smokes," I said. "How?"

Pop chuckled to himself. "No one ever discovered how."

"Did they catch it?" I asked him.

"Oh yes, they caught it," said Ma. "Outside my bedroom window!"

"Jeepers," said Ace, crunching on his toast. "All the best stuff happens to your family."

CHAPTER 3

WHEN I POINTED OUT THAT KEEPING ME IN THE house all summer would be more work for her, Ma changed her mind pretty quick. Plus, today was Saturday, and I shine shoes at Pop's shop on Saturday mornings. So she sprang us right after breakfast.

"But don't go near that zoo!" she hollered after us.

"Don't worry, Ma," I called over my shoulder.

I waited on Ace's front porch while he ran inside and got dressed. It wasn't like I couldn't go in, but it was cooler outside, and besides, whenever I go into that house, Ace's little sister tries to talk me into playing some goofy board game. Plus, she cheats. I've learned that it's best to wait outside.

A minute later Ace came out, eating a banana. He hadn't bothered to comb his hair.

"I still can't believe I slept through the whole polar bear caper," he said as we walked up the sidewalk toward the zoo.

I couldn't help bragging a little. "You know what they say: The early bird gets the worm."

He snorted. "Who cares about worms?"

"Never mind."

Three blocks later, there it was. We could already see a bunch of people gathered in front of the bear dens. We skirted around to the front of the crowd, which was mostly kids, a few fellas with notebooks and pens talking to Mr. Stankey, the head zookeeper, and even a couple of police officers.

And there was Frosty, neck-deep in his swimming hole. He looked like he was wondering what the big deal was, and by the way, did anyone bring any fish?

"What are you two knuckleheads doing here?" said a voice behind us.

I knew that voice. It belonged to Pete Costas.

Here's what you need to know about Pete: He's big, and he's mean, and he's been beating me up on a regular basis since second grade.

The problem is I can't avoid him. I see him at school every day. At Greek school too, which is only once a week, but even that's too much, if you ask me. Thank goodness it was finally summer vacation. But I'd still have to see his ugly mug in church every Sunday. I sure hope God is paying attention, because I should get credit for putting up with Pete Costas.

I took a deep breath and turned around. "What're you doing here, Pete?"

"I can be here if I want!" he said. "The zoo is public property."

"Is that so?" said Ace, sidling up to Pete (who was almost twice his size). "Looks like Frosty wasn't the only smelly animal to escape from his cage today." Pete's the kind of kid Ace loves to pick a fight with. Big but slow. One of these days, it's going to get Ace into big, slow trouble.

Pete loomed over Ace and balled his hands into fists. "You're lucky there's coppers right over there," he growled. "Or else you'd be Frosty's breakfast by now. You know how he loves marshmallows."

"Who're you calling a marshmallow?" said Ace, taking a step closer to doom.

"Hiya, fellas!" said another familiar voice.

It was Penny, who's a friend of ours, even though she's a girl. She's a grade behind me, but taller, which bugs me a little, but she can't help it. She's also a really good baseball player, which makes up for all the other stuff.

When they saw Penny, Ace and Pete forgot about trying to kill each other. Penny has that sort of effect on people.

Maybe it's her height, or the way she can blow a bubble almost as big as her head. But mostly it's because Penny can strike out any batter on three pitches. That's the kind of skill that earns you respect around here.

"Hiya, Penny!" said Ace. "Did you hear what happened? Frosty escaped!"

"I know. Hiya, Pete." She blew a bubble.

"Get lost," said Pete. He turned and pushed his way through the crowd.

"What's up with him?" Penny asked, watching him go.

Ace made a face. "Got lost on his way home to the reptile house. Come on, let's go see what Mr. Stankey's saying."

"I bet those guys with notebooks are newspaper reporters," said Penny.

She was right. When we got closer, we could see a tag on one fella's chest that said JOURNAL. Another fella had a card in his hatband that read SENTINEL, and the third one's tag said CHICAGO TRIBUNE.

"Look at that!" I whispered. "There's a reporter here all the way from Chicago!"

The *Journal* reporter was asking a question. "How's the milkman doing, Mr. Stankey? Will he recover?"

Mr. Stankey sighed. "The milkman is fine. There's nothing to recover from, except maybe a bit of a startle. I'm told he finished his route and is on his way home for a rest." Mr. Stankey pulled at the collar of his khaki shirt. For someone who was going to be in the newspapers, he did not look like he was having much fun.

The *Tribune* reporter pushed forward. "You're in charge of the zoo, Mr. Stankey. How did the polar bear get out?"

"That's a good question," answered Mr. Stankey, almost to himself. "As head zookeeper, I personally make the rounds of the entire zoo every night before going home. I can assure you that last night, all the animal enclosures were locked up tight."

The *Tribune* fella scribbled in his notebook. "Would you say that this sort of thing was bound to happen, Mr. Stankey? I mean, there's no fence around this zoo. No gates. No admission fee. People can come and go as they please, any hour of the day or night. And so can the animals, evidently!"

"This zoo is part of the city park," explained Mr. Stankey. "The good people of this city are entitled to free access to their park."

The *Journal* reporter chimed in. "What about the animal enclosures? How can the public be sure they're safe, when there's nothing but a dry moat between them and a huge beast with fangs and claws?"

"Do you see that moat?" said Mr. Stankey, sounding a little hurt. "It's too wide to jump across. And the sides are too steep to climb. I'm telling you, it's impossible for an animal to escape under normal circumstances."

The *Sentinel* reporter perked up. "Are you saying that the polar bear had help? Can I quote you on that?" He scribbled in his notebook.

"No, you can't!" said Mr. Stankey. "I have nothing more to say at this time." And he squeezed past the reporters, looking a little pale.

But it did make me wonder: How *did* Frosty get out?

"I got it!" said Ace. "I know how I'll never miss another escape from the zoo!"

"How?" said Penny.

"A paper route!"

I scoffed. "You? Wouldn't you have to get up at four in the morning?"

"That's the whole point!" he told me. "My ma's been bugging me to get a summer job, right? If I got a paper route, she'd be happy, and I'd be out in the neighborhood every day, early. I'd never miss any of the good stuff ever again!"

"You'd miss some good sleep," I said. "Besides, how do you know the good stuff will always happen at four in the morning?"

"I don't know that," said Ace. "But if it does, I'll be ready. Where will you be? In bed, getting your beauty sleep."

Penny laughed out loud. "I'd like to see what you'd do if you saw a polar bear coming up the sidewalk!"

Ace's ears turned red. "Oh yeah? I was gonna invite you

along one morning, so you could see all the excitement for yourself. But now maybe I won't." He kicked at the grass. "I'm gonna go find out how I can get a paper route. See you two later." And just like that, he stomped off.

Which reminded me. "Holy smokes! I gotta get to Pop's shop!"

And I left poor ol' Penny standing there with no one to talk to except Frosty.

CHAPTER

4

ACE GOT HIS PAPER ROUTE, ALL RIGHT. HE EVEN snagged the perfect territory: all the streets around the south side of the park, including our street, and Mr. Stankey's office at the zoo. As it happened, the kid who already had that route had just quit. Apparently, he didn't want to be out by himself, in the dark, roaming the same streets as marauding polar bears. His loss, if you ask me. But he was only too happy to turn over the whole route to someone else. So on Monday, Ace started his very own paper route.

He lasted five days.

"This stinks," said Ace on Friday morning after he'd finished his deliveries. We were sitting on the steps of his front porch. His hair was sticking up. His shirt was buttoned crooked, and his shoes were coming untied. I couldn't tell if that's what happens when you get dressed at four in the morning, or if he'd had an incident while he was delivering papers. I gotta admit, I was afraid to ask.

"My back hurts," Ace groaned. "My feet hurt. My shoulders hurt. Do you know how much a satchel of newspapers weighs? Oh sure, they suck you in by starting you on a Monday. Monday's edition is the skinniest of the whole week! I tell ya, if you ever want to rob a bank, do it on a Sunday, because all the reporters are taking the day off. So you go along for a few days, and by Wednesday you figure it's not so bad. But then on Thursday—BAM! The ad supplement. That makes the paper twice as thick and heavy. And I have to bundle all the sections myself before I even start delivering!"

I wanted to point out that banks are closed on Sundays, so even the bank robbers take the day off. But I got his point about the Monday versus Thursday editions.

Just then, Penny walked up. She tilted her head at Ace. "What's the matter with you? You look like you fell out a window."

Ace groaned.

"The new paper route," I told her. "Feet hurt, shoulders hurt, Thursdays are the ad supplement." And now Penny was pretty much caught up.

"Oh." She sat down on the steps with us. "How about using your bike? Maybe that'll make things easier."

"I tried that," said Ace. "I kept falling over from all that weight. And the dogs! Don't even get me started about the dogs."

"But Ace," I said, "if dogs are giving you trouble, what're you gonna do when you see a polar bear?"

"That's another thing," said Ace. "Not a single polar bear all week! I've been getting up in the middle of the night for nothing!"

Penny tried being sensible. "Maybe you shouldn't get your hopes up. What are the chances Frosty will escape again?"

"What were the chances the first time?" he asked. Which, I had to admit, was hard to argue with.

Penny blew a bubble and fiddled with her hair ribbon. As usual, it was losing the fight against her cloud of black hair. "How many papers do you deliver?"

"Sixty," he moaned. "Every single day, including Sundays. What was I thinking?"

Being his best pal, I realized it was my job to cheer him up. "Tomorrow is Saturday," I reminded him. "You get paid tomorrow, right?"

"Yeah," he said, perking up a little. But then he sagged again. "I'll have to go around twice tomorrow—once to deliver the papers, and a second time to collect from all the customers once they're awake. Including the ones with dogs. I have to pay for all the newspapers out of that money, and I only get whatever's left! And now that my ma knows I'm doing something useful, she won't let me quit. This stinks." He dropped his head onto his knees.

Penny and I looked at each other and shrugged. What else can you say to a guy who already looks like he fell out a window?

Penny knew what to say. "Can I help?"

Ace's head popped up. "Help what?"

"What do you think? The paper route. I could go along with you tomorrow, to learn the route. And then next week, we'll each take half the route, and be done in half the time. We'll split the pay fifty-fifty."

Ace wiped his nose on his sleeve. "You'd do that for me?"

She shrugged. "I wake up at four every morning anyway, 'cause that's what time my dad leaves for work."

Penny's dad is a motorcycle cop. He rides a huge Harley, which you can hear from two blocks away even when he doesn't rev the engine. One time he let me and Ace take turns sitting on it. I'm not even embarrassed to be seen in front of a girl's house, as long as I can be seen sitting on a big ol' police-department-issued Harley.

"I've never heard of a girl with a paper route before," I said. "Is that allowed?"

Ace shrugged. "It'll be four in the morning. Who's to know?"

"Ace is right," said Penny. "Gee whiz, Nick. You worry too much."

"I'm not worried," I said, even though something about the whole idea bothered me. "I know you'll do a great job, Penny."

Ace perked up. "So do I," he said. "Penny, you're hired."

CHAPTER

5

THAT'S HOW I ENDED UP GOING TO SPARKY'S CUSTARD Shop by myself on Saturday.

Sparky's is Uncle Spiro's custard shop. He opened it about a month ago, and he's really proud of that place. He goes early every day to polish it up and admire how nice it looks. He's doing good business, too. In fact, he's so busy that he hired me to work for him every Saturday afternoon. That's where I'd be hanging out anyway, so I might as well get paid.

I was already working for Pop every Saturday morning, shining shoes. He owns the Elegant Shoe Repair and Hat Shop downtown. I don't mind it. I get good tips, and it's better than doing chores around the house for Ma. And believe me, she wouldn't even pay me.

So it all works out okay.

Today, I was home from Pop's by noon, but Ace and Penny still hadn't come back from collecting for their paper route. So I had to walk up to Sparky's on my own.

The shop was busy, even for a Saturday. You'd be surprised how many people eat frozen custard for lunch.

"What's shakin', squirt?" said Uncle Spiro as I walked in.

"Nothing." I grabbed an apron off the peg and a broom from the corner. It's my job to sweep the floor and wipe off the tables and countertop. You'd also be surprised at what slobs people can be. I know I was.

Spiro finished serving a customer, and then he came out from behind the counter. "Where are your pals?"

I kept sweeping. "Out. Making collections. They're sharing Ace's paper route."

"You don't say," said Uncle Spiro. "Penny, on a paper route? Good for her."

"I guess."

"How come you're being such a sad sack?" Then he gave me a squint. "You're not jealous that they're delivering papers and you're not, are you?"

"Heck no!" I stabbed at a crumb on the floor.

"What are you sore about, then?"

I stopped sweeping. I was sore, all right. But I didn't really know why.

Apparently, my mouth did, because it started working

all by itself. "It's the second week of summer vacation, and I never see Ace. He's up early every day, and then he goes home to take a nap, and I'm stuck on my own until after lunch. And now Penny's doing it too. I knew this would happen as soon as they started that stupid paper route!"

Spiro scratched his head under his soda-jerk hat. "Aren't you shining shoes every Saturday morning anyway?"

"Well, yeah," I admitted. "But Ace used to come in and keep me company. It's so boring with only Pop to talk to. They haven't seen a polar bear once, by the way. They're not *going* to see a polar bear! This was supposed to be the best summer ever. But it's already the worst."

And that's how I found out what I was sore about.

Uncle Spiro put a hand on my shoulder. "Don't worry. Give 'em a chance to get used to their new routine. Besides, Ace can't stay away from here for long. Not when he gets all the free custard he can eat, which is a lot, by the way."

He was right, I guess. At least, I hoped he'd be right. Summer vacation gets boring in a hurry when you have no one to be lazy with.

The bell over the door jangled as more customers came into the shop.

"Chin up," said Uncle Spiro, and he scurried back behind the counter.

Just then, Ace and Penny finally came busting in.

"Hiya, Uncle Spiro!" hollered Ace. "Hiya, Nick! Did ya miss us?"

"Nope," I lied, jabbing the broom along the floor.

"Hi, Mr. Spirakis," said Penny.

"Call me Uncle Spiro," said Uncle Spiro from behind the counter. "Say, Penny, how's that beautiful sister of yours?"

He was talking about Penny's big sister, Josie. Josie *is* beautiful, I guess. Not that Penny isn't beautiful. I don't know, maybe she is, but I can't tell, on account of she's my pal and so I never really thought about it. Anyway, the best thing about Josie is that she's a professional baseball player. She pitches for the Kenosha Comets of the All-American Girls' Professional Baseball League. Uncle Spiro said he'd take me and Ace and Penny down to Kenosha sometime this summer to watch one of Josie's games. We'll see if that ever happens now, what with that stupid paper route.

"Josie's fine," said Penny. "She says hi."

"Does she?" said Spiro, grinning like a fool. "Well, you tell her hi back!"

"I will."

"All right already," interrupted Ace. "Can't a fella get a scoop of chocolate around here?"

Spiro grabbed a cone and dug a huge scoop of custard from the bin. He made a big show of handing the filled cone to Penny, and then he looked Ace up and down. "What happened to you? Run over by a dump truck?"

Ace's shirt was buttoned wrong again, half untucked, and wrinkled. He had twigs in his hair.

"It took us all morning to collect," he said. "It's amazing how many people suddenly aren't home when you're asking for money. We had to go around twice. The second time, Penny knocked on the doors while I hid in the bushes. Boy, were those folks surprised to see a girl collecting for the paper." He licked his lips and looked at Penny's cone like he might melt away to nothing if he didn't get custard pretty soon.

Uncle Spiro took pity on him. He scooped out two more cones of chocolate and handed them over to me and Ace.

"This is the best custard in the whole wide world," said Ace between slurps. "What's your secret ingredient?"

"As if I'd tell you," said Uncle Spiro with a wink. "Did all your customers finally pay you?"

"All except five," said Ace. He pulled a little notebook out of his back pocket and smoothed out the rumples. "I'm keeping track, too, because if someone doesn't pay, that's money out of my pocket."

"Our pockets," Penny reminded him. She took a delicate lick of her cone. Somehow, Penny can eat an entire cone of frozen custard without dripping any of it onto herself.

"Speaking of pockets . . ." Ace dug out about a zillion coins and some crumpled bills and plunked it all on the counter.

"Jeepers, that's a lot of coins," I said. I can never stay sore at Ace for long.

"No kidding," said Ace. "I could hardly keep my pants up."

"Good thing nobody's dog chased you today," I told him.

He checked his notebook. "I figured it out last night: If all my customers pay me, I should get eighteen dollars. And then I have to pay the route supervisor thirteen fifty for the papers. That leaves four fifty for me."

"Us," said Penny.

"Right." Ace counted out $13.50 from his pile of money and pushed it aside.

"Here ya go, sport." Uncle Spiro handed Ace an empty pint-sized tub and a paper bag with SPARKY'S CUSTARD stamped on the side. "Nobody wants to see your underwear."

Ace dumped the $13.50 into the tub, put the lid on, and stuck the whole thing into the paper bag. Then he counted the coins that were left.

"Three dollars." He slapped his notebook onto the counter. "I'm short a buck fifty!" He slumped onto his stool. "Here, Penny. I owe you half."

"Nah," said Penny. "You did the whole route yourself this week. I only went around one day." She took another dainty lick of her cone. Not a drop of custard anywhere. I don't know how she does it.

Ace relaxed. "That's real swell of you, Penny." He started scraping his money off the counter.

"How about fifty cents?" Penny held out a spotlessly clean hand.

Ace stopped midscrape. "That's fair," he admitted. "I wouldn't have collected hardly anything if you hadn't come with me." He handed her two quarters.

Penny pocketed her money. "We'll figure out a way to collect that dollar and a half."

"You got that right," answered Ace. He tapped the notebook with a finger. "Those people still owe us money, and I know where they live."

CHAPTER

6

W E'D HARDLY FINISHED OUR SECOND CONES WHEN trouble walked in.

"Well, well, well!" said trouble in a loud voice. "If it ain't ol' *Sparky*! Or should I say, it *ain't* ol' Sparky, 'cause there's no such *person* as Sparky!"

A few customers looked up from their cones, possibly wondering if this news should ruin their enjoyment of frozen custard. Apparently, it didn't, because after a few seconds they went back to slurping.

Spiro shot a glance toward the door. "What're you doing here, Happy?"

Happy Harold owns a custard stand of his own a couple of neighborhoods over. It's been there forever. His custard is actually pretty good, but ironically, Happy is never actually happy.

He's been even less happy since Uncle Spiro opened his shop. Happy Harold claims that Spiro is trying to steal his customers. Which is ridiculous, because Happy's shop is all the way on the other side of the park. Plus, if you ask me, there are plenty of customers to go around.

"Sometimes a fella needs a break," he said, strolling around the shop. "I been meaning to pay you a visit, but I been so *busy* lately. But don't worry, I left my employees in charge. You know what employees are, Sparky? It's people you *pay* to work at your shop 'cause you're so *busy*, and making so much *dough*, that you need a little help." He swept a finger along the countertop and inspected it for dust and goo. I happen to know he came up with nothing, because I scrub that counter till it gleams. You could eat off that counter. Some people do, too. I've seen it.

Spiro waved a hand in my direction. "What about Nick here? He sure looks like an employee to me."

I stood up tall and straightened my apron.

Happy snorted. "That kid? What is he, twelve? The only reason a kid that age can even *work* for you is 'cause he's family. I bet you pay him peanuts, too. Am I right, kid? Or does ol' Sparky pay you in custard?"

I lifted my chin. "He pays me in custard *and* in money." Mostly custard, but that was none of Happy Harold's business.

"We're doing just fine, Happy," said Spiro. He slid open the top of a freezer chest and pulled out a carton of custard. "A pint of vanilla. On me." He slipped the tub into a SPARKY'S CUSTARD paper bag and set it on the counter. "If you want to know what custard is *supposed* to taste like."

Happy did not touch the bag. He just looked at it like it smelled funny. "Prepacked, huh? If that's your idea of *quality*. Or maybe you're giving your fancy new machines a rest. Yeah, those King Kustard machines are awful touchy. Breaking down all the time. Personally, I use Conemaster machines. But that's just me. Nothing but the best for my shop."

"You're wearing out your welcome, Happy," grumbled Spiro.

Happy Harold raised his voice again. "Gee whiz, I'm thirsty. Mind if I get a drink of water at your *bubbler*?"

Happy was getting on my nerves. "There's no bubbler," I piped up. "Folks don't come in here for water. They come for the custard."

"No bubbler?" said Happy. "That's too bad! In my experience—my *long* experience—folks can work up quite a thirst while eating custard. *If* the custard's any good." He gave a sniff toward the paper bag, which was still sitting on the counter.

"I hate to say this, Nick," Ace whispered, "but all of a sudden I'm thirsty."

"Then don't say it!" I hissed, even though all of a sudden I was thirsty too.

Uncle Spiro wasn't thirsty. He was mad. "What're you trying to say, Hap? Out with it already."

Now Happy was really enjoying himself. "Oh, haven't you heard? I just had a brand-new *bubbler* installed in my shop. All the ice-cold water you can drink, anytime you want it."

There was a general murmuring around the shop. A few people gulped and looked around, as if a bubbler might appear out of nowhere because all of a sudden they were thirsty too.

Happy couldn't stop rubbing it in. "Of course, it *cost* me a pretty penny. But that's just me. I know how to take care of my customers."

Happy Harold and Uncle Spiro glared at each other. No one said a word. No one breathed. I swear I could hear the clock on the wall ticking.

That's when I stepped right up to Happy Harold and said, "Sparky's custard is ten times better than yours." And then I said as casually as I could: "Must be his secret ingredient."

I hadn't planned on saying that. It just jumped out. If Pop were here, he'd ground me for a year for mouthing off to a grown-up like that. But I was mad. Uncle Spiro worked hard to make Sparky's a success, and Happy Harold had no business coming in here trying to mess that up.

For a second, I thought Happy was gonna punch me. But he just stood there, fuming. For once, Happy Harold couldn't think of anything to say.

Other people could, though. Now the words "secret ingredient" were swirling around the shop like leaves on a windy day. A few people even got back in line for seconds. No one looked one bit thirsty anymore.

Behind the counter, Uncle Spiro whistled a tune and scooped custard as fast as he could.

All this made Happy pretty furious. He grabbed his paper bag and stormed out of the shop.

Uncle Spiro kept on whistling.

CHAPTER 7

WE KEPT OUR MOUTHS SHUT UNTIL THE DOOR jingled closed behind Happy.

"That was spectacular!" said Ace. He nudged me. "So there *is* a secret ingredient? I knew it! What is it?"

I shrugged. "I only said that because Happy made me mad."

But Ace wasn't buying it. "Uncle Spiro!" he said. "What's the secret ingredient?"

Spiro looked up from making change. "It wouldn't be a secret if I told you, would it?" And he gave a wicked grin. I couldn't tell if that meant he was pulling Ace's leg, or if there really *was* a secret ingredient. Either way, it drove Ace bonkers.

Penny finished off her cone and wiped her squeaky-clean fingers on her squeaky-clean napkin. "I didn't taste anything except chocolate."

But now Ace had the idea stuck in his head. "Maybe it's in the vanilla," he guessed. "Hey, Uncle Spiro! Can I have a cone of vanilla?"

"Get in line," said Uncle Spiro. "Behind the paying customers. And from now on, I'm cutting you off after three cones."

"Jeepers," grumbled Ace. "I'm only trying to help." And then he walked to the back of the line to order his vanilla cone.

"Well?" I said after he'd finished slurping it down.

"Beats me," he said. "Unless 'delicious' is an ingredient. I think vanilla is my new favorite flavor."

Uncle Spiro said, "I think your favorite flavor is 'free.'"

Finally everyone was served and Spiro could take a breather.

"Well?" said Ace. "What's the secret ingredient? We won't tell."

Uncle Spiro looked around to make sure no one else was listening. He leaned over the counter and motioned us closer.

And then he grinned again. "I'll tell you later."

That made me sit up straight. "You mean there really *is* a secret ingredient?"

Uncle Spiro just kept grinning.

Penny nudged Ace and pointed to the clock on the wall. "Don't you have to pay for your newspapers before three o'clock?"

Ace gasped. "Holy smokes, you're right! Okay, we'll go as soon as we hear the secret ingredient." He turned back to Uncle Spiro.

Penny tapped her foot. "We'll have to run all the way there as it is," she said. "You don't want to get fired after only one week, do you?"

Ace shuddered. "I'd never hear the end of it from my ma. Come on, Penny." He grabbed his paper bag off the counter and headed for the door. "Uncle Spiro, don't say anything until we get back!"

The door had barely jingled shut behind them when I leaned across the counter and whispered to Spiro, "Well? What's the secret ingredient?"

Uncle Spiro cocked an eyebrow. "What about Ace and Penny?"

"Are you kidding? Ace can't keep his mouth shut. If you told him, the whole town would know by tomorrow. I'll tell Penny later."

Spiro grabbed a clean rag and started polishing the custard machines.

I tried again. "Please? I'm family!"

He stopped in midpolish, and I knew he was crumbling. "Okay," he said, setting down his rag. "We gotta be quick, though. I can't leave customers waiting."

He led me around to the little storage and washing-up room behind the custard machines. After a few seconds of pushing things around on a shelf, he pulled down a big ol' brown glass jug and unscrewed the top. "Take a whiff of this," he said.

I sniffed.

I jumped back. My eyes watered. It smelled sort of like custard, but . . . stronger. Like custard would smell if it could punch you in the nose.

But it reminded me of something else, too. What was it? I braced myself and took another careful whiff.

And then I got a picture in my head of Pop, on special occasions like Christmas or Ma's birthday, sitting in his chair and sipping on something brown.

My mouth dropped open. "Whiskey?"

"Shhh!" Spiro screwed the top onto the jug and put it back on the shelf. But he was laughing.

"What's so funny?"

"Nothing," he said, but he was still laughing. Just then, the bell on the shop door jingled. "I gotta get back up front."

A little while later, here came Ace and Penny, back

from making their first weekly payment to the newspaper supervisor.

"That was fast," I said. "You've been gone for hardly ten minutes."

It had been a rough ten minutes. Ace's shirt was still untucked, wrinkled, and buttoned wrong. Somewhere along the way, he'd managed to rip the knee of his pants. And he was still carrying the paper Sparky's bag with the money for the route supervisor, which for some reason was looking soggy.

Even Penny was a mess. Her spotlessly clean overalls were not spotless anymore. She'd lost her hair ribbon. She and Ace were both breathing hard, like they'd run the whole way there and back.

Which of course made me think of one thing.

"The polar bear got out again?"

"No, you knucklehead!" Ace slammed the paper bag onto the counter. It did not go *clink*. It went *splurt*. "Custard!"

I was still confused. "What about custard?"

Penny stepped forward and opened the bag. She pulled out a pint carton and held it up with two fingers. It was . . . dripping.

"Vanilla," she said.

"What happened to your tub of money?" I said.

Ace actually growled. I thought Penny was gonna throw a pint of half-melted custard at me.

Uncle Spiro said, "Ohhhhh."

"Wait a minute," I said. "Is that the pint of custard that Uncle Spiro gave to Happy Harold?"

All three of them nodded slowly.

"But I saw him walk out of here with a bag."

They nodded again.

And that's when I finally figured it out.

"Holy smokes. Happy Harold walked out of here with Ace's newspaper money!"

CHAPTER

"HAPPY HAROLD STOLE MY MONEY!" HOLLERED ACE.

"He didn't steal it," said Penny, but then her eyebrows bunched. "Did he?"

"It must've been an accident," I tried. "Happy's a sourpuss, but he's not a thief. I don't think."

"I need that money," moaned Ace. "If I don't pay for my newspapers, I'll get fired. I can't get fired after my first week!"

"Calm down, everyone," said Uncle Spiro, who has to say that kind of stuff because he's a grown-up. "Are you sure it's not still here somewhere?"

We searched the entire shop for Ace's paper bag, but it was gone.

Penny dusted herself off. "That does it. We're going to Happy's."

Ace followed her toward the door. "Wait'll I see that Happy Harold."

"I'm coming with you!" I pulled off my apron and tossed it to Spiro. At times like this, a fella needs his best pal. Besides, I really wanted to see the look on Happy Harold's face when Ace and Penny walked into his shop looking for their newspaper money.

"I feel awful about this, fellas," said Uncle Spiro, even though it wasn't his fault. He opened his cash register and dug out three dimes. "Take the streetcar. It's a long way to Happy's, and you look like you could use a break." He was mostly talking about Ace, of course.

"Thanks, Uncle Spiro. We'll let you know what happens." I took the dimes and we headed out the door.

"Do you think Happy will be there?" asked Penny while we waited for the streetcar.

"He'd better be," said Ace. He was trying to sound tough, but he looked a little green around the gills.

"You feeling okay?" I asked him.

"I'm feeling just swell," he said. "Considering I've been up since four a.m., walked a paper route three times, ate three huge cones of custard for lunch, ran twenty blocks, and tore my pants. Oh, and I'm out thirteen fifty."

"We'll get it back," said Penny. "I hope."

The streetcar pulled up. We all piled on and found a seat at the back.

And then I thought of something that would cheer Ace up. It was going against my better judgment, but if you'd seen Ace right then, you wouldn't blame me. "Guess what?" I said. "I found out the secret ingredient in Sparky's custard!"

That did the trick.

"Let's hear it!" said Ace.

I glanced around to make sure no one else was listening. "Promise you won't say anything to anybody."

"I promise," said Penny. "Cross my heart."

"Wild polar bears couldn't drag it out of me," said Ace.

They both leaned in close so I could whisper the word.

"Jeepers!" said Penny after I told them. "Honest?"

I nodded. "Saw it and smelled it for myself."

"No kidding?" said Ace. "Whiskey?"

"Shhhhhh!!"

Penny pushed the hair out of her eyes. "But Sparky's custard doesn't taste like whiskey. I know it's a secret ingredient, but if it's so secret you can't even taste it, what's the point?"

I'd been thinking about that. "I watched my ma in the kitchen one time," I said. "Did you know that she puts cinnamon in her spaghetti sauce?"

Ace's eyes got wide. "Nah, you're pulling my leg. I've had your ma's spaghetti sauce, and I never tasted any cinnamon."

"That's the whole idea," I told him. "The secret ingredient is *in* the food, and it makes the food taste better, but you can't taste the actual ingredient. Because it's secret. Or something like that."

Ace groaned. "I can't believe I ate three giant scoops of whiskey."

Penny squinted at him. "Do you feel drunk?"

"I dunno," he said. "Is feeling drunk the same as feeling like you ate too much and then ran twenty blocks?"

"I don't think so," I said. "I think you just ate too much and then ran twenty blocks."

Penny nudged us. "This is our stop." She pulled the signal cord and we all jumped off the streetcar.

Things were really hopping at Happy's. A long line of people waited on the sidewalk to order at the walk-up window, and the outside picnic tables were full. (Like I said, Happy does make good custard. And like I also said, there are plenty of customers to go around.)

We pushed our way through the crowd. Happy wasn't working at the walk-up window, so we elbowed our way inside.

No sign of him behind the counter, either. There was only a big, dark-haired kid, whose back was turned.

"Hey, soda jerk!" said Ace to the kid behind the counter. "Where's Happy?"

The kid turned around and leaned over the counter

toward Ace. "Who you calling a jerk, you little runt?"

I didn't think Ace could look any more pale than he already did, but I was wrong. Because the big kid behind the counter was Pete Costas.

"What are you doing here?" I squeaked.

Pete turned his beady eyes on me. "What's it look like, genius? I work here. You think I'm wearing this getup because I like it?" He gave us a look that dared anybody to say that Pete Costas liked wearing a bow tie, apron, and soda-jerk cap.

Ace didn't take the hint. Or maybe he didn't care. The color came back to his cheeks, and he said, "No, Pete. It's a little early for Halloween, that's all."

I don't think Ace would've said that if there hadn't been a counter separating him from Pete, and a whole shop full of potential witnesses.

"Jeepers, Ace," I hissed. "We're here to get your money back, remember?"

"Look!" said Penny, tugging at my sleeve. "The bubbler."

There it was, in the back corner of the shop. A white porcelain pedestal and bowl, with a shiny brass spout and handle.

All of a sudden I was very thirsty.

Ace and I dared each other with our eyes to be the first to take a drink. Then, before either of us could make a move, Penny stepped up, turned the handle, and took a big slurp of clean, cold deliciousness. "Ahhhhh."

The shoving match between me and Ace lasted half a second. Ace is small, but he's fast, so he usually wins these battles. Plus, he bites. But this time I won.

That was the first hint that something was really wrong with Ace.

But I couldn't resist the bubbler. I took a good long drink.

"Hurry up!" said Ace. "I'm parched here!"

"Well, well, *well*," said a voice behind us. "How do ya like that *bubbler*, kids?"

Happy Harold.

All three of us turned and stood at attention, as if we'd been caught doing something we weren't supposed to be doing. But that was stupid. We had every right to be there, drinking Happy's free water.

Ace got straight to the point. "You have my newspaper money."

For a second, Happy looked honestly confused. Then realization dawned, and he said, "So *you're* the kids who keep their loose change in a pint-sized *custard* tub."

Penny gasped. "You *do* have Ace's money!" She crossed her arms. "Well, he wants it back. Thirteen dollars and fifty cents."

"Thirteen *fifty*?" said Happy. "Gee, that's a lot of dough to leave lying around for anybody to walk off with. You could buy a couple *hundred* cones with that! A fella could get *sick* eating that much custard!"

That might have been the wrong thing to say. Ace's face went all pasty again.

I stepped forward. "Give my friend his money back."

He looked me up and down. "Well, if it isn't Sparky's *employee*. You kids want your money back? I want something in exchange." He loomed over us. "Tell me Sparky's secret ingredient."

That Happy sure had a lot of nerve.

"We aren't telling you any secret ingredient," I said.

"That's right," said Ace, who was looking really pale now. He shook a wobbly finger at Happy. "If you think we're gonna tell you about that whiskey—"

I'll bet you could hear the gasp from out on the street. Even Ace looked surprised to hear what had just come out of his mouth.

Behind the counter, Pete let out a snort.

Happy grinned his slimy grin. "Whiskey, eh?" He tapped his foot and rubbed his chin. Then he reached around behind the counter and pulled out a paper bag with SPARKY'S CUSTARD stamped on it. "A deal's a deal. Give my regards to *Sparky*."

And then a lot of things happened all at once.

Penny snatched the paper bag out of Happy's hand.

I blurted, "You haven't heard the last from us, Happy!"

And Ace bent over and barfed all over Happy's shoes.

CHAPTER 9

YOU'D BE SURPRISED AT HOW FAST A KID CAN RUN immediately after throwing up. But Ace kept up with me and Penny like his life depended on it, and maybe it did.

We bolted out the door of Happy's custard stand and straight onto the streetcar, which, in a stroke of lucky timing, happened to be waiting at the corner. We jumped aboard just in time to see Happy busting out onto the sidewalk, fuming mad, and all his customers scrambling out of the way of his stinky shoes.

"Are you okay?" Penny asked Ace. She wrinkled her nose. "Sit over there."

Ace sat in an empty seat across the aisle from me and Penny. Even friendship has limits.

"I feel great!" he said. To be honest, he looked much better than he had only a couple of minutes ago. The color had come back to his face, and he was grinning from ear to ear. I guess he was relieved in more ways than one.

"Yeah, well, don't feel *too* great," I said. "Now we have to tell Uncle Spiro that Happy Harold knows his secret ingredient!"

Ace went pale again. "Sorry. I don't know what came over me."

I snorted. "You're a blabbermouth, that's what came over you. *You* can tell Uncle Spiro what happened."

"We'll all tell him," said Penny. "We're a team."

That Penny is a real peach. A team. I liked the sound of that.

She settled the Sparky's bag onto her lap, and this time it went *clink* instead of *splurt*. "But first we'll stop off and pay for Ace's newspapers."

So that's what we did. Ace did not get fired, once he explained the mix-up and turned over his $13.50. The route supervisor said, "All's well that ends well," and reached out to ruffle Ace's hair, but then he got a whiff of Ace and backed off in a hurry.

By the time we got to Sparky's, the dinner crowd was starting to gather. There are plenty of people in this town who consider frozen custard to be a nutritious meal: You've got your dairy, your eggs, and—if you order a banana split—your fruit. Uncle Spiro is not about to argue with any of those people.

Normally, Ace would be one of those folks, but that night we had to practically drag him inside, and not only because he didn't want to face Uncle Spiro. He held his nose and whimpered, "No more custard!"

"How'd it go at Happy's?" said Uncle Spiro when he saw us coming in. Then he made a face. "What's that smell?"

Penny changed the subject. "Happy did have our money. And he gave it back! Ace paid for his newspapers and everything."

"How about that?" said Spiro. "I didn't think ol' Happy had a generous bone in his body."

"He doesn't," I said. "He only gave it to us in exchange for . . . information." I grabbed Ace's sleeve to keep him from slinking away.

Uncle Spiro gave us a suspicious look. "What kind of information?"

Penny and I both looked at Ace. Ace gulped and tried not to look at Spiro.

"Horace," said Uncle Spiro. "You have something to tell me?" Ace hates it when people use his full name. Spiro knows it, too.

Ace was looking a little pale again. "I think I need some fresh air."

"Tell him," I said. "Then you can go outside."

Ace looked longingly at the door. He squeezed his eyes shut, blurted, "I told Happy about the whiskey," and bolted outside. The last time I saw him, he was bent over a trash can.

But Uncle Spiro wasn't mad. As a matter of fact, he started laughing.

"What's so funny?" I said. "We spilled the beans about the secret ingredient to your worst enemy, and you're laughing?"

"I'm laughing because whiskey is *not* the secret ingredient." He filled a couple of cones and handed them to the next customer in line.

"That big brown bottle in the back of the shop!" I said. "That's not whiskey?"

"Sorry about that, sport," said Uncle Spiro, but he didn't look very sorry. "It's vanilla extract."

I didn't get it. "It sure smelled like whiskey."

"That's because vanilla extract is made with alcohol. The vanilla beans soak in it. Everybody uses a few drops of it in their custard."

"So it's not a secret?" I said.

"Nope." He shrugged. "There is no secret ingredient. But promise me you won't tell Ace. You were right, Nick. He can't keep his mouth shut."

"Okay, I promise," I said.

"Me too," said Penny.

Just then, the bell over the door jingled. It was Ace, looking healthy again. "I'm back. What'd I miss?"

CHAPTER
10

PENNY AND I KEPT OUR PROMISE TO UNCLE SPIRO. We did not tell Ace that there was no secret ingredient.

"You didn't miss anything," I said.

Ace tried again. "Penny?"

"Not a thing."

"Uncle Spiro?"

"Nothin'."

Poor Ace. I really wanted to tell him. But it was for his own good. I think he knew it too, because he dropped the subject and sat there looking pathetic. Or maybe he'd finally gotten a good whiff of himself.

Behind us, the door jingled open again.

"Well, if it ain't ol' Flapjack!" said a booming voice.

Spiro's eyebrows shot up, and a huge grin spread across his face. "Sarge! You ol' son of a gun! You finally made it!" He hustled out from behind the counter and pumped the visitor's hand.

This Sarge fella was huge. I thought his handshake was gonna lift Uncle Spiro right off the floor. "It's a swell place ya got here, kid! Will ya look at all these happy customers!"

"I owe it all to you, Sarge," said Uncle Spiro. "Hey, kids, let me introduce you to a real VIP. You've heard of South Side Lenny? Well, here he is, in the flesh. Lenny, this is my nephew, Nick, and his pals Ace and Penny."

We all waved politely.

Penny said, "How come Uncle Spiro calls you Sarge?"

"We were in the war together," boomed Lenny. "I was his sergeant, and ol' Flapjack here was my best hashslinger." He slapped Uncle Spiro on the back, practically knocking him down. Spiro didn't seem to mind one bit.

"Hashslinger?" said Ace, looking impressed. "What's that? Machine gunner?"

"Cook," said Lenny.

"That's right," said Uncle Spiro. "And once the war was over, Lenny taught me everything he knows about the frozen custard biz."

South Side Lenny followed Spiro behind the counter. "These King Kustard machines sure are beauties, aren't they? Cost an arm and a leg, I'll bet."

"They're worth it," said Uncle Spiro. "I would've settled for Conemaster machines if it wasn't for you. I don't care what Happy Harold says."

Lenny lifted an eyebrow. "What did Happy Harold say?"

Uncle Spiro shrugged. "Nothin'. He stopped in earlier today, bragging about Conemaster machines and bubblers."

"That's Happy for ya," said Lenny, shaking his head. "He makes the rounds of all the custard shops every once in a while, to show off and to spy on the competition. He paid me a visit last week." Lenny buffed a shiny custard machine with his sleeve. "I hope I haven't steered you wrong. I've had two King Kustards myself for years and never had a lick of trouble. Until now. As a matter of fact, that's one reason I'm here. I need a favor."

"Name it, Sarge," said Spiro. I got the feeling that if South Side Lenny asked Uncle Spiro to stand on his head in front of everybody, Spiro would do it, no questions asked.

"Well, it's like this," said Lenny. "Every summer, Mr. Stankey at the zoo hires me to run his custard concession. It's nothing big. Just a little freezer cart that I can wheel around and sell prepacked cups, ya know? But one of my machines broke down last week. First time ever! Now I'm down to one machine, and I can't make enough custard to serve my customers at the shop and supply the zoo cart. I was wondering if you could help me out? Take over the zoo concession for the summer?"

Custard? The zoo? Two of the best things in the whole world, together in the same place?

"He'll do it!" I said without even thinking.

Uncle Spiro lifted an eyebrow at me. Then he said, "Gee, Sarge, that's real nice of you, but I'm sure you'll get your machine up and running in no time."

"That's the other problem," said Lenny. "The machine needs a new part, made to order. It'll take three weeks at least."

Uncle Spiro scratched his head. "Wouldn't you rather ask someone with more experience?"

Lenny waved him off. "You have all the experience you need. Besides, I already got the thumbs-up from Charley Stankey. The job is yours if you want it. You'd be the only frozen custard cart at the zoo."

"No kidding?" said Uncle Spiro.

"That's right," said Sarge. "Happy Harold's been wanting for years to open a second cart at the zoo, but Charley Stankey won't hear of it. He says the zoo doesn't need two custard vendors." He chuckled. "Happy's developed a real sore spot for Charley Stankey."

Uncle Spiro frowned. "Gee, Sarge. I don't want to get on Happy's bad side."

"Face it, Flapjack," said Sarge, giving him another slap on the back. "You've been on Happy's bad side since the day you opened this shop. What do ya say?"

This was it. My chance to have the best summer ever. Ace and Penny could keep their dumb ol' paper route. I tried again. "Say yes, Uncle Spiro. It'd be swell!"

Spiro held up a hand so we'd be quiet and he could think. "I'd have to hire someone to run it," he said.

Here was my chance. "Hire me," I told him. "I can run it!"

"Thanks, Nick, but you're not old enough," said Uncle Spiro. "There's a city ordinance. You have to be fourteen to be in charge."

"Why not use the kid I hired before my machine went bust?" said Sarge. "Billy's all thumbs sometimes, but he's a good kid."

"Gee, thanks, Sarge," said Uncle Spiro. He cocked his head in my direction. "What about hiring a twelve-year-old helper?"

I held my breath.

"Sure thing," said Lenny. "You're the boss! You'll do great business, especially with the Fourth of July coming up. The busiest day of the year. Everyone will get to know Sparky's custard. Come on, what do ya say?"

We all stared at him, waiting.

Uncle Spiro nodded slowly, and I could see a smile creeping onto his face. Finally he offered his hand to South Side Lenny. "Okay, Sarge. Count me in."

CHAPTER 11

I COULDN'T BELIEVE MY GOOD LUCK. IN ONE LONG day, the summer had gone from the worst ever to the best ever. Penny and Ace could have their dumb paper route. I had Sparky's Frozen Custard Cart at the zoo. If anyone was gonna see an escaped polar bear, or any other excitement involving wild animals, it'd be good ol' Nick Spirakis, with a front-row seat.

To celebrate, I got a chocolate cone for the road. Then we all said so long to Uncle Spiro and South Side Lenny and headed home for supper (and in Ace's case, a good hosing down).

Ace made a face as we walked. "How can you eat that stuff?"

"I'm hungry," I explained between slurps.

"It's almost suppertime," said Penny. "Won't your mother be mad?"

"Nah," I said. "She's used to it."

On the way home, we took a detour through the zoo. We wanted to get a peek at the custard cart.

"I'll bet it's in the storage shed behind Mr. Stankey's office," said Ace. "He keeps all the good stuff in there."

I wanted to ask what "the good stuff" was, and how Ace knew where it was kept, but I let it slide.

Sure enough, we could see the cart through the window of the darkened shed. A white freezer chest, mounted on a metal frame between two bicycle wheels. It had a handle across the back for pushing it, and a big umbrella attached to one side. The front and side of the chest were painted with red lettering:

SOUTH SIDE LENNY'S

FROZEN CUSTARD

THE BEST IN TOWN!

"You'll have to change that," said Penny.

"Piece of cake," I said. "We'll paint a couple of signs and hang 'em on top of Lenny's lettering."

"Where do you suppose is the best place to set up a custard cart?" said Penny, looking around.

That was a good question. "Anywhere, I guess," I told her. "It's on wheels, so you can push it around."

Ace shook his head. "If it was me, I'd pick one spot and stay put. So people would always know where to find me."

I had to hand it to Ace. Every once in a while, he actually made sense.

"Okay," I told him. "Where would that be?"

"That's easy," said Ace. "Monkey Island."

I thought about that for about half a second. "Horace," I said, shaking my half-eaten cone at him, "sometimes you're a genius."

"Don't point that thing at me," he said, wrinkling his nose. "Let's go take a look." So we walked over toward Monkey Island.

We found a patch of grass near the main zoo entrance, in the shade of a big tree. We could see Frosty's enclosure in one direction and the snack pavilion in the other direction. And there was Monkey Island across the path. Everyone who visited the zoo would end up in this spot sooner or later. And that meant everyone would see Sparky's Frozen Custard Cart. Ace was right: It was the perfect spot.

"Look!" said Penny, pointing down at the watery moat that surrounded the island. "One little monkey is swimming this way. You're sure it can't climb out?" She took a step back.

Penny was still pretty new in town, so she wasn't used

to being this close to the zoo animals. I explained it to her the way the zookeeper had explained it to me and Ace one time. "The moat is shallow where it touches the island. But it gets deeper here at the outer edge. The monkeys can't touch the bottom, so they can't jump out. And the wall is too smooth for them to climb. So there's nothing to worry about. At least, there hasn't been anything to worry about since 1929, according to my ma."

Penny leaned over the fence and reached toward the water. "I can almost touch it," she said.

"Don't!" said Ace. "You might fall in. And those monkeys bite." I won't go into details right now, but let's just say he knew all this from personal experience.

He nudged me as the little monkey swam closer. "See if it likes frozen custard. Toss it a chunk of your cone."

I shook my head. "What if a zookeeper catches me?" But that monkey was making a beeline toward us, and I could swear he was eyeing my cone.

"Just a tiny little chunk," said Ace. He looked around. "No one's watching."

I had to admit, it was tempting. Now the monkey was swimming back and forth at the edge of the moat, looking up at us like we had the only food in the whole wide world. It was so close, I could see two little dark patches of fur above its eyes, like fat eyebrows. It reminded me of Pop.

Ace nudged me again. "Come on. He looks hungry!"

"She," said Penny.

"Huh?"

Penny pointed. "That monkey is a girl."

Both me and Ace squinted at that monkey, but to be honest, we weren't even sure what we were looking for. Half of it was underwater, for one thing. Besides, it's not like monkeys wear clothes or put ribbons in their hair.

"How do you know?" said Ace.

Penny shrugged. "I don't. I just decided that she's a girl."

"Okay, smartie," I told her. "What's her name?"

Penny tilted her head and squinted at that little monkey, thinking. Finally she said, "Her name is Maxene."

"Why?"

"Why not?"

Girls. I don't get 'em.

Just then, the last of my cone got snatched out of my hand and landed in the water of the moat.

"Ace!"

"I didn't do it!" Which meant (of course) he did.

Quick as lightning, Maxene the monkey reached out, grabbed the cone, and took a nibble.

And then she squealed and tossed that cone right back over the fence. It almost hit Ace in the back of the head.

"What the heck?" said Ace, while me and Penny snorted with laughter.

"I guess Maxene doesn't like custard," said Penny, wiping her eyes.

"Or maybe she doesn't like chocolate," I suggested. "I hope you learned your lesson, Ace."

"Yeah, yeah," he said. "Do not feed the animals."

"No," I said. "Never turn your back on a monkey."

"Hey, you kids!" hollered a voice behind us.

"Yikes!" said Ace. We all took off before the zookeeper could catch us.

I should've been mad at Ace for almost getting us into trouble, but I couldn't help smiling as I ran home. This was shaping up to be a swell summer after all.

CHAPTER

12

AFTER SUPPER, I NABBED A BAG OF MARSHMALLOWS from the pantry and walked back to the zoo by myself.

This was my favorite time of day. It wouldn't be dark for another couple of hours, but most of the zoo visitors had gone home to eat dinner and to sit on their front porches with the ball game on the radio.

The zoo animals were settling in too. I bet they were relieved to finally have the place to themselves. If I had a houseful of visitors all day, chattering and making faces and watching my every move, I know I'd be glad to see them leave.

I ate a couple of marshmallows and wandered up the path, past Mountain Goat Mountain and the rhinoceros yard, where Tank the rhino was patrolling his perimeter. Tank looks fierce. He *is* fierce. He could trample me flat without even trying, which is why I never go into his yard unless it's absolutely necessary. But most of the time he just strolls around his yard, or rolls in the dirt, or sleeps under a tree, and he only eats grass and leaves and stuff. I plucked a handful of clover from the grass at my feet and pushed it through the fence so he could reach it. And I then I walked over to check on Frosty.

There he was in his enclosure, napping in the shade. I'll bet he was glad that the heat wave was finally over. I can sleep in my underwear when it's hot, but Frosty is permanently stuck in that thick fur coat.

Right now, his fur looked yellowish in the evening light, and when the breeze blew, I could see his black skin peeking through his fur. Did you know that all polar bears have black skin? A zookeeper told me that. So actually, Frosty was not a white bear. He was a black bear with white fur. It just goes to show you: What you see on the surface is not always the whole story.

It had been a week since Frosty busted out. I chewed on another marshmallow and wondered: Did Frosty think about things differently, now that he'd seen the outside world? Did he like what he'd seen and hope to visit again sometime? Or had he decided that it wasn't worth the bother?

And why did he bust out in the first place? Was he bored? Lonely? Maybe he was looking for other polar bears. Or maybe he just wanted to go for a walk. If I was stuck in my house all the time, I'd feel like busting out too, sooner or later.

You might think I'm goofy for trying to figure out what was going on inside an animal's head. But let me ask you: What else is the zoo for? It sure isn't for the animals. You can't tell me that Frosty is happier here, cooped up in this city park thousands of miles from his real home. Sure, he's fed and safe, and he has an easy life. But he never actually decided to live in a zoo. In fact, I'm pretty sure that no one asked any of these animals if they wanted to live in a zoo. Nope, zoos are not for animals. Zoos are for people. The least we can do is feel grateful to all these critters for giving up their normal lives so that we have something interesting to look at on a summer day.

No one else was around, so I tossed a marshmallow in Frosty's direction. It sailed over the moat and landed just out of his reach. He opened one eye. Then he rolled over, stuck out his long tongue (which was also black), and lapped it up.

I knew I shouldn't have done that, especially after I'd hollered at Ace for throwing my custard to Maxene the monkey. Plus (of course), it's officially against the rules. But the zookeepers don't bother to enforce them. Or maybe it happens so often that they can't keep up.

Anyway, like I said: Frosty might have an easy life, but it's not really a good life. If you ask me, he deserves a marshmallow every now and then.

CHAPTER

13

THE NEXT DAY WAS SUNDAY. FOR ONCE, I DIDN'T mind going to church. In fact, I was in such a good mood, I decided I would not make faces at Pete Costas. Plus, I'd try and stay awake for the whole thing.

I almost made it. But I must've dozed off at the end there, because one minute the cantor was singing, and the next thing I knew, everyone was making for the exits.

Ma and Pop didn't say anything. They were probably just happy that this time I didn't snore.

When we got home, Uncle Spiro was reading the Sunday paper in his pajamas and slippers. He has an agreement with Ma and Pop: He doesn't go to church, and they . . . come to think of it, I guess they don't have an agreement. Uncle Spiro just doesn't go to church.

"How's things downtown?" he said as we walked in.

"If you want to know what happens at church, you should find out for yourself," sniffed Ma, taking off her hat and gloves.

I bailed him out. "Sophie Costas was looking for you again."

He made a face. "Sorry I asked." Sophie Costas is Pete's big sister. She has eyes for Uncle Spiro, who does not like her, but she won't take a hint. Come to think of it, that's probably one reason he doesn't go to church.

Pop put his fedora in the closet and smoothed his hair. "How is the frozen custard business?" he asked. "You came home very late last night."

"Saturday's my busiest night," said Uncle Spiro, folding the newspaper. "The joint was really jumpin'."

"A jumping joint is good, *neh*?" said Pop. He's not up to speed on all the American slang.

"It's very good," said Spiro. And then he told Ma and Pop all about South Side Lenny stopping by and the frozen custard cart at the zoo.

"I'm gonna help out," I said. "But don't worry, Pop. I'll still come to the shop and shine shoes every Saturday morning, like I promised."

Pop settled into his armchair and picked up the front section of the paper. "I'm proud of you both for working so hard. But, Nicky, what about baseball?"

That was a good question. Up until a couple of weeks ago, me and Ace and a bunch of the fellas played ball every day at the zoo. But then there was this batboy contest down at the ballpark and things got . . . a little crazy. It involved lying, forgery, a punch in the eye, and being chased by a rhinoceros. And that was just me. Anyway, the whole episode put a damper on our team spirit.

But all I said was, "We're taking a break from baseball for a while."

Pop nodded sympathetically. "How about Ace?" he said. "Why I haven't seen him in the shop lately?"

I found the comics and plopped onto the rug. "He's doing a paper route with Penny every morning."

Ma switched on the radio and settled into her chair. The Andrews Sisters were singing "Pennsylvania Polka."

"Nicky," she said, "did you say Penny is doing a paper route? She's the nice girl with all the hair, *neh*, who plays baseball?"

"That's her," I said.

Uncle Spiro reached for the Sports page. "I bet that arm of hers is coming in handy now that she's tossing newspapers onto porches every morning."

"I guess," I said. I was happy for Penny. Honest.

"I never hear of a girl delivering the newspapers," said Ma.

"Me either," I told her. "But that's Penny for ya."

"Hmmm," said Ma. I wasn't sure she'd heard me. Her eyes were closed, and she was tapping her foot to the music on the radio.

Pop turned a page of his newspaper. "It's not right for the girls to do boy things. Not ladylike."

I guess Ma was paying attention after all, because she opened her eyes and said, "What means 'ladylike,' George? It does not mean 'crippled' or 'weak.' Good for Penny. I like that girl." She closed her eyes again.

"It's not right," said Pop again. "The women must be dainty. It is for the men and boys to do the heavy jobs."

"Ha!" said Ma, who was wide awake now. "Who carries the washing up from the basement to hang outside to dry? Who walks home from the market with the groceries? If the women waited for the men to do all the heavy jobs, no one would eat or have anything to wear."

She had a point. One time, she made me carry a basketful of wet towels up the basement stairs. It was so heavy, I almost fell over. Come to think of it, if Ma challenged me to an arm wrestle right now, I'd run the other way.

"Spiro," said Pop, in a hurry to change the subject, "who will run your custard cart at the zoo? You will need to hire someone, *neh*?"

"I'll hire this kid that Lenny knows," said Uncle Spiro. "And Nick here will be his right-hand man."

"Good boy, Nicky," said Pop, and I couldn't help sitting up a little straighter, even though he called me Nicky, which is a baby name.

"Who is this kid you are hiring?" said Ma.

Spiro shrugged. "Some kid named Billy. I'm sure he'll be fine."

Ma drummed her fingers on the arm of her chair, thinking. "Do you know his mother?"

"I don't think so," said Uncle Spiro. "Does that matter?"

She shrugged and closed her eyes again. "They always try harder if they know you can call their mother."

CHAPTER

14

MONDAY MORNING AT BREAKFAST, UNCLE SPIRO gave me a dollar and sent me to the five-and-dime to buy paint and poster board for new SPARKY'S signs. Then he headed to the shop early to start making extra custard.

"Hiya, squirt," he called when I walked in later that morning. The shop wasn't open yet, and he was busy scooping custard into little wax-paper cups, fitting them with lids, and stacking them in the chest freezer. A fella in overalls was behind the counter too, digging around inside a giant red toolbox.

"Everything okay back there?" I asked. I set down the painting supplies and handed Uncle Spiro his change.

"Everything's hunky-dory," said Spiro. "Isn't that right, Eugene?"

The fella in overalls gave a thumbs-up without looking around.

Uncle Spiro filled another cup with custard. "Eugene here is from the King Kustard company," he said. "After South Side Lenny told us about the trouble with his machine, I figured I'd better get mine checked out, just in case. I don't want any surprises."

"Don't you worry," said Eugene, straightening up and cleaning his hands on a rag. "Both of your machines are fit as a fiddle. They'll last twenty years at least."

"Glad to hear it," said Uncle Spiro. "Good ol' Lenny never steered me wrong."

"Funny thing about Lenny's machine," said Eugene. "I never seen anything like it. It had a big dent in it—almost like someone took a hammer to it or something."

Uncle Spiro gave him a worried look. "That *is* funny," he said. He didn't mean ha-ha funny either.

"Oh, it's nothing that can't be fixed," said Eugene. "It was prob'ly one of them teenagers who work for him. I bet one of 'em dropped something, or knocked into it, and was scared to own up to the boss. You know what them kids are like. Too busy flirting with the girls to watch what they're doing." Eugene finally noticed me standing there. "Not you, though, son. You look like you're too smart to flirt with any girls." He winked.

I cleared my throat and pretended my face did not

feel hot. "You got that right," I muttered.

Eugene closed his giant toolbox and headed for the door. "No charge for today. Call me anytime."

We watched him drive off in his truck. Finally I said, "What do you suppose really happened to South Side Lenny's custard machine?"

Spiro flipped the sign on the door from CLOSED to OPEN. "I dunno. It probably happened the way Eugene said. You know what you kids are like. Always flirting with the girls." He nudged me with an elbow, and then he ambled back behind the counter.

"I'm serious," I told him. "What if somebody did it on purpose?"

"On purpose? Who would do that?"

I knew exactly who would do that. "Happy Harold."

Uncle Spiro gave me the stink-eye. "What makes you say that?"

"Remember what South Side Lenny said the other day? That Happy Harold came around his shop last week? And Lenny's machine just happened to go bust last week too. Like someone took a hammer to it, Eugene said."

Uncle Spiro washed his hands. "I dunno. Sabotaging Lenny's custard machine? Happy's a little cranky, but I don't think he'd do anything like that."

"Happy Harold is more than a little cranky," I said. "He only gave Ace his newspaper money because we accidentally told him your fake secret ingredient. Even after he knew it was Ace's money. That's pretty mean, to take a kid's money."

Uncle Spiro shook his head. "What'd be the point of wrecking one of Lenny's custard machines? To steal his customers? He'd have to wreck both of Lenny's machines, not just one."

"Maybe he was going to wreck both machines but got interrupted before he had the chance."

"So you're a detective now?" said Uncle Spiro. "Okay, Sam Spade, let's say you're right. That still wouldn't guarantee more customers for Happy Harold. People could just as easily come here, or to any other custard stand in town. Happy'd have to wreck everyone's machines."

"Lenny did say that Happy Harold likes to make the rounds of all the custard stands," I told him. "And wasn't he eyeing your machines? Bragging about how King Kustards are always breaking down, or something like that?"

Uncle Spiro scoffed. "You've been listening to too many detective shows on the radio, Nick. Besides, you heard Eugene. My machines are fit as a fiddle."

He had a point. But something smelled fishy. One way or another, I'd find out what had really happened to South Side Lenny's custard machine.

I couldn't wait to tell Ace and Penny. This was big news. Bigger than a stupid paper route. Bigger than hoping for another polar bear escape. But I'd forget about all that and invite them to help me investigate this mystery. Because, like Penny said the other day, we were a team.

That's when Ace came busting into the shop, all out of breath. His face was red, and—I know this will come as a shock—he was a mess.

"What the heck happened to you?" I said. "I thought you'd be home, taking your stupid nap after finishing your stupid paper route." (Except I didn't actually say the word "stupid" out loud.)

"I haven't even been home yet!" he gasped. "I ran all the way from the zoo!"

I looked him over and took a guess. "The polar bear escaped again and chased you?"

He shook his head and gulped a breath. "Worse," he said. "Happy!"

"The polar bear chased Happy?"

"No!"

I was really confused now. "Happy chased you?"

"No!" Ace stumbled over to the counter. "Uncle Spiro, how soon can you get your custard cart up and running?"

"I'm aiming for Friday," said Uncle Spiro, pointing to the stack of wax-paper cups waiting to be filled.

"But it's only Monday!" said Ace with his usual knack for the obvious.

"So?"

"Happy!" said Ace again. "Happy set up his own custard cart at the zoo!"

Uncle Spiro dropped his scooper with a clatter. "What?"

"It's true," said Ace, still breathless. "There's a Happy's Frozen Custard Cart, right under that big tree at the main entrance to the zoo."

Uncle Spiro scowled. "That Happy sure has a lot of nerve."

"Can he do that?" I said. "South Side Lenny said you'd be the only custard cart at the zoo. Happy doesn't have Mr. Stankey's permission!"

"I'll bet he's not officially on zoo property," said Uncle Spiro. "Which means he doesn't need Mr. Stankey's permission."

"Yeah, well, he's spittin' distance from Monkey Island," said Ace. "You gotta get your cart out there, Uncle Spiro, before people get used to seeing Happy Harold."

And then, as if things weren't crazy enough, in came Penny, and she was all red in the face too. "You won't believe what happened at the zoo!" she gasped.

"Ace already told us," I said.

She looked at Ace in surprise. "I didn't see you there."

"I didn't see you there either," said Ace. "Anyway, I already told them about Happy's custard cart."

Penny's eyes got wide. "Happy has a custard cart?" Then she waved everything away and started over.

"Anyway, that's not my news." She sat down at the counter to catch her breath. Uncle Spiro handed her a cup of water, and she drank it while we patiently waited for her to finish up already.

Finally she set down the empty cup and said, "Remember when the polar bear escaped from the zoo week before last?"

"How could we forget?" I said.

"Well, guess what?" she said. "He didn't *escape* after all. Somebody *let* him out."

CHAPTER

15

I STOOD THERE WITH MY MOUTH HANGING OPEN. "Somebody let Frosty escape on purpose?" This was big news. Really big news.

Even bigger than Happy Harold's sneaky custard cart.

Way bigger than a possibly deliberately damaged custard machine.

I should have been excited.

I *was* excited. Honest.

"What were you two doing at the zoo this morning, anyway?" I asked. "What about the paper route?"

"The zoo is on my half of the route," explained Penny proudly.

"I always take a shortcut through the zoo on my way

home," said Ace. "But when I saw Happy's cart, I came straight here." He suddenly looked worried. "I missed breakfast."

Uncle Spiro scooped vanilla custard into a cone and handed it to Ace.

"I thought you were off custard," I said.

Ace looked at me like I was crazy, and slurped his cone.

"Start from the beginning, Penny," said Uncle Spiro.

Penny settled onto her stool at the counter. "I was delivering the paper to Mr. Stankey's office at the zoo, like I do every day. Nobody was around yet except for a couple of zookeepers, but they didn't even notice me. They were too busy picking up yesterday's trash."

I knew what she was talking about. There are plenty of trash barrels at the zoo, but you'd be surprised how much litter ends up on the ground, and even in the animal enclosures. One time I watched the zookeepers cleaning out the Monkey Island moat. They filled an entire wheelbarrow with trash, including soda bottles, candy wrappers, small tree branches, a baseball with a torn cover, and one shoe. Like I said: People can be real slobs.

Penny kept going with her story. "The zookeepers started talking about the polar bear. One of them said that on the morning Frosty escaped, his back door was found open!"

"Frosty has a back door?" said Ace.

I thought about that. "Frosty has a back room, right? Where he sleeps? There must be a door from that room out to the real world. So the zookeepers can bring Frosty his food and give him his checkups and stuff like that. They sure as shootin' don't climb through the moat."

"That must be the door that was left open," said Penny.

Ace wiped his sticky fingers on his shirt. "We need to find that back door."

"Hold your horses," said Uncle Spiro. "This is all very exciting, but if I want to get my custard cart up and running ASAP, I need some signs painted PDQ."

He was right. We decided to divide and conquer. Ace would go spy on Happy Harold's sneaky custard cart. Penny would nose around the zoo to see what she could find out about Frosty's back door.

And I'd . . . stay at Sparky's to paint signs.

"We'll meet back here in an hour?" I said.

"Perfect," said Ace. "Lunchtime." And they headed out the door.

✳ ✳ ✳

That's how I got stuck painting signs all by myself, which was a bad idea. I don't know what it is with me and paint, but we do not get along.

Uncle Spiro knows this, so he sent me out to the alley behind the shop with the poster boards and paint. It turned out to be the right move. At least most of the spilled paint ended up on the pavement and not on me.

Half an hour later, I had three signs painted, and they looked pretty darn good. They all said SPARKY'S FROZEN CUSTARD in big blue letters. (Well, one of them said CUSTERD instead of CUSTARD and also had paw prints going across it. Somewhere out there is a nosy cat with blue feet.)

I brought the signs in to show Uncle Spiro. He glanced over and gave a thumbs-up but couldn't say anything because he was on the phone.

"Is that so?" he was saying. "Golly, that's too bad. Well, I'm glad he's okay. That's all right, I'll find someone. Okay, Sarge. Thanks." And he hung up.

"Those signs look swell," he told me, but he hardly looked at them.

"I can fix the one that says 'custerd,'" I said, in case that would help. "There was this cat . . ."

"That's okay, no one will notice," said Uncle Spiro. I wasn't sure *he'd* noticed.

"Everything okay?" I asked.

"That was South Side Lenny," said Spiro. "I called him to ask if that kid Billy would be able to start working the custard cart tomorrow. But Lenny said that Billy had a . . . a mishap."

"What kind of mishap? Is he okay?"

"He sprained his ankle. Slipped and fell on the ice."

I blinked. "It's June."

Uncle Spiro shrugged. "Something about unloading a bucket of ice cubes for Lenny's soda fountain and spilling it all over the floor. Anyway, Billy won't be able to work the custard cart."

I felt bad for Billy, I really did.

But who needed Billy, anyway?

"Are you sure I can't run the custard cart?" I said. "I'd be good at it."

Uncle Spiro scooped custard for a waiting customer. "Thanks, Nick. I wish you could, but there's that city ordinance. Don't worry, we'll find someone else. I hope." Then he finally took a good look at my signs. "Hey, those look swell! Except 'custard' is spelled wrong on that one."

So much for no one noticing.

CHAPTER

16

JUST THEN, THE BELL ON THE DOOR JINGLED, AND in walked Ma. She brings lunch for Uncle Spiro on most days. It saves him from having to close up shop at lunchtime, and also from eating nothing but custard all day.

"Hiya, Athena," said Uncle Spiro. He loves Ma. Probably because she lets him live with us, even though he's grown up and could be living on his own.

Ma wrestled her little two-wheeled shopping cart through the front door. "Today I bring leftover spanakopita and some nice noodles."

As I already mentioned, Ma's spaghetti (with that secret pinch of cinnamon in the sauce) is pretty darn delicious. And the leftovers are just as good.

"Just in time," said Uncle Spiro. "I'm starving."

The door jingled again and some customers came in for their lunchtime custard. "Go ahead and start," he told us. "Save some for me."

Ma and I went to the storage room behind the custard machines, where Uncle Spiro keeps a folding table and chairs. I unloaded the cart while Ma took off her hat and gloves.

"I see you are getting ready for doing your business at the zoo," she said, nodding toward the SPARKY'S FROZEN CUSTARD signs, which were propped up around the room while the paint dried. Then she looked again and squinted. "Why that one has little blue footprints?"

"There was a cat behind the garbage cans," I explained. At least she didn't notice CUSTERD. For once I was glad that Ma couldn't read English very well.

"Anyway, we gotta get ready as quick as we can," I told her. "Happy Harold already set up his own custard cart!"

Ma made a face. "I thought Spiro was the only person allowed to sell custard at the zoo."

"He is," I said. "Happy Harold is skirting the rules."

"What kind of person does that?" said Ma, crossing her arms. "Rules should not have skirts!" For a second I thought she was going to stomp over to give Happy Harold a piece of her mind. I would've paid good money to see that, by the way.

"I know it, Ma, but Uncle Spiro says there's nothing we can do, except get our own cart out there right away." And then I remembered. "Except now we don't have anyone to run the cart."

Ma handed me a plate of noodles. "What about the boy Spiro was going to hire?"

"Billy? He hurt himself. Slipping on the ice!"

"Ice?" she said. "It's June!"

"I know! Anyway, Billy's out of commission. And I'm not old enough, according to Uncle Spiro. So we need to find someone else." I sat down and tucked a napkin into my collar.

"Hm," said Ma. "When the zoo cart will be open?"

"Every day, from noon till five," I told her. "We wanted to start tomorrow."

Uncle Spiro walked in and washed his hands at the sink. "Sounds like Nick told you about our problem, Athena."

"Someone named Happy is putting skirts on the rules, and someone named Billy is ice-skating in June," she said. She drummed her fingers on the table. "What your cart person needs to do, Spiro? Scoop the custard, *neh*?"

Spiro sat down to lunch. "He won't even have to do that. I'm filling the cups ahead of time. He'll only need to hand out the cups and spoons. Collect money. Make change. That's about it. Nick can run between here and the zoo, with supplies and stuff."

Ma squinted at him. Finally she said, "Maybe I know somebody."

"You do?" he said, sitting up straight. "Who?"

"A respectable member of our church," said Ma. She cocked an eyebrow. "If you ever went to church, you might know this person, but since you don't . . ."

He was too excited to get suckered into that old argument. "I don't care who it is as long as he's responsible and at least fourteen years old."

"Sure, sure," said Ma, waving a hand. "All of those things."

"I'll pay the going rate, of course. Do you think he could start tomorrow?"

Ma shrugged. "I will find out. At the zoo, *neh*? At noon?"

"Right," said Uncle Spiro. "We'll be set up between Monkey Island and the polar bear den. He can't miss it." Just then, the shop door jingled again. Spiro sighed, set down his fork, and got up from the table. "You're a lifesaver, Athena. I owe you one."

Ma shooed him out and said, "I know."

CHAPTER

17

AFTER WE FINISHED LUNCH, MA PUT ON HER HAT and gloves. I followed her to the front of the shop.

"Bring the dishes home later, Nicky," she said. "After Spiro eats." She grabbed my chin and kissed my cheek. I hate it when she does that.

"Okay, Ma." I rubbed lipstick off my face as she headed out the door.

A few minutes later, Ace and Penny showed up.

"We're back!" announced Ace. "Something smells good." He followed his nose toward the back room and dove at Uncle Spiro's untouched plate like Frosty pouncing on a marshmallow.

"What did you find out at the zoo?" I asked them.

"I think I found Frosty's back door," said Penny. "Right around the corner from Monkey Island. It's a heavy steel door with a big ol' lock and a sign that says 'No Public Admittance.'"

"That must be it!" I said. "How about you, Ace? What's Happy Harold up to?"

"He wasn't there," he said through a mouthful of food. "Out to lunch, a sign said. So I tried peeking inside his cart. But it was padlocked. Padlocked! That Happy Harold sure is suspicious." He took another bite.

"What's that?" said Penny, pointing daintily at the spanakopita.

"It's a kind of spinach and cheese pie," I said. "My ma made it."

"I've never seen anything like that before," she said. She licked her lips.

"Want some?"

She nodded, so I scooped some of it onto a clean plate, being careful not to get my fingers bitten as Ace went in for seconds.

Penny took a polite nibble of the spanakopita.

"It's delicious!" she said, and she took a bigger bite this time. She got some crumbs on her chin, but she didn't seem to care. It was the first time I'd ever seen Penny with food on her face. It was swell.

That's when Uncle Spiro came in. "Finally, I can sit down and eat!" He pulled up a chair and looked around for his plate. And there was Ace, shoveling the last of the food into his mouth.

"That was my lunch!" said Uncle Spiro.

Ace's ears turned red. "Oops." And then he burped.

Uncle Spiro stared at Ace and shook his head. Then he sighed, reached into his pocket, and took out a dollar bill. "Run and get me a sandwich from the deli around the corner. Corned beef and Swiss. Extra mustard. And I want my change back."

Ace took the money without a word and headed toward the door.

"How do you like Nick's signs, Penny?" said Uncle Spiro.

She looked them over. She did not mention CUSTERD, which was very polite of her. She even said, "Great idea to decorate that one with paw prints, Nick. It's perfect for the zoo," which was also very polite.

A few minutes later, Ace was back from the deli.

"I got you a pickle, too," he said, handing Uncle Spiro a paper bag and his change. Then he sat down and yawned.

Uncle Spiro unwrapped his sandwich. "What's the matter, Ace? Still not used to getting up before the crack of dawn?"

Ace yawned again. "I don't know what I was thinking, getting a morning paper route."

"You were thinking you'd see an escaped polar bear," I reminded him.

"Well, that was dumb," he said. "The whole thing is dumb—getting up at four in the morning, walking miles with that heavy sack over my shoulder. Trying to collect money from people who don't wanna pay. Scary dogs. No polar bears."

"It's only been a week," I told him.

Ace groaned. "Only a week?"

"It's not so bad," said Penny. "I kind of like it."

Ace perked up. "I'm glad to hear you say that, Penny. In fact, I've been meaning to ask you something." He coughed. "What do you think about taking over my half of the route?"

She blinked at him. "You mean, do the whole paper route myself?"

"Sure, why not?" said Ace. "You just said you like it. Plus, you're good at it. You never throw newspapers into puddles. Dogs never chase you. And people are so surprised to see a girl collecting for the paper that they actually pay you."

Penny thought about it. "It *is* fun tossing papers onto porches. I'm teaching myself to throw a curveball!" Good ol' Penny. A ballplayer through and through.

"See?" said Ace. "Doesn't it work out swell for you?"

Penny gave him a funny look, but she was also half smiling. "I need to ask my folks," she said. "But I think it'll be okay with them."

"Gee, thanks, Penny," said Ace, looking relieved. "That works out swell for me, too, because I already told my ma I quit."

CHAPTER

18

ACE COULDN'T WAIT TO TELL HIS MA THAT HE'D found someone to take over his paper route. "You fellas want to come with me? Help me give her the good news?"

I knew what that meant. "She's not done hollering at you for quitting, is she? And you're hoping she won't holler at you in front of us."

Ace's ears went red. "Something like that."

"You can't blame her," said Penny. "Quitting after only a week."

"I know," said Ace, "but I didn't think I'd hate it this much."

We all got cones for the road, said so long to Uncle Spiro, and headed out toward Ace's house.

"Speaking of hollering," said Penny as we walked,

"what did your route supervisor say when you quit?"

Ace coughed. "I haven't told him yet." He kicked a pebble along the sidewalk.

"Scared?" I said.

"Am not!" said Ace. "Besides, now I can tell him I already found someone to replace me, so he can't be too sore about it. Can he?"

"You don't think he'll mind that a girl is taking over your route?" said Penny.

Ace kicked the pebble again. "As long as the papers get delivered, and he gets paid for them, why should he care?"

"Some people care," said Penny, but that's all she said.

That made me remember what Pop had said the other day—that girls should be ladylike and dainty. Was Penny unladylike? To be honest, I'd never really thought about it one way or the other. Penny was just . . . Penny. She could toss newspapers as well as any boy could. Better, probably. It didn't seem fair, being told what you could and couldn't do, just because you were a girl.

That made me kind of feel sorry for Penny.

I'd never say that to her face, though. She's bigger than me, and she probably could beat me up.

Ace's ma was outside, digging in her garden. She was wearing a big straw hat and old shoes that didn't match. I like Ace's ma. Despite what Ace says, she hardly ever hollers.

"Hello, kids!" she said when she saw us coming up the walk. "Are you enjoying your summer so far?"

We all nodded politely, even Ace.

"That's nice," she said. "Say, Nick, how's your uncle's frozen custard business?"

"It's doing swell, thanks," I told her.

"Good for him!" she said. "We'll have to stop by sometime. That reminds me: Horace, I'm glad you're home. I have some wonderful news for you!"

"Now what?" said Ace.

"You know how you wanted to quit your paper route?" Ace's ma turned to me and Penny. "Horace wanted to quit his paper route, but his father told him, 'Not so fast, young man. A summer job is good for you. It builds character. You'll make a bit of money. You'll get out of the house!' And then, you'll never guess what I saw at the market today. Right there, on the bulletin board at the Red Owl, a 'Help Wanted' notice. 'Summer only,' it read. 'Energetic boy for frozen custard business.' Can you believe the luck? Why, it's perfect for you, don't you think, Horace?"

For once, Ace was speechless.

His ma made up for it. "The address was written on the notice, so I decided to stop by on the way home and inquire for you. No time like the present, I always say! I thought it might have been your uncle's shop, Nick."

But I knew it couldn't have been Sparky's, because

Sparky's Custard Shop was nowhere near the Red Owl.

In fact, there was only one frozen custard shop anywhere near the Red Owl.

Happy Harold's.

Holy smokes.

"It wasn't your uncle's shop after all, Nick," said Ace's ma. "It was a place called Happy's. Do you know it?"

I thought Ace was going to faint right there in the petunia patch.

Nothing came out of my mouth except a squeak.

Penny stepped up to the plate. "Oh, yes, ma'am, we know Happy Harold, all right."

"Isn't that nice!" said Ace's ma. "I told him all about you, Horace—especially how energetic you are—and he said you're exactly what he needs for his new custard cart. At the zoo! He hired you on the spot. You can start tomorrow. Isn't that wonderful?"

CHAPTER

19

AND THAT'S HOW ACE ENDED UP WORKING FOR Happy Harold.

Ace was not happy about working for Happy, for obvious reasons. I wasn't crazy about it either. The only good thing about it was the chance to see the look on Happy's face when he found out he'd hired the kid who'd barfed all over his shoes.

The next day, while Ace went to meet his fate at Happy's cart, Penny and I carried the new SPARKY'S FROZEN CUSTARD signs to the zoo.

"How's the paper route?" I asked her. "Your first morning on your own!"

"It was good!" she said. "Don't tell Ace, but I think it

went faster without him. And the newspaper shack was so busy that no one even noticed a girl picking up bundles of papers. I think I'm gonna like it."

"That's swell!" I told her. Good ol' Penny.

Inside the storage shed behind Mr. Stankey's office, we dusted off the custard cart and hung the SPARKY'S signs on the sides. A few minutes later, Uncle Spiro showed up with my old red wagon full of prepacked cups of custard and some chunks of ice.

"This is a nice surprise, Penny," he said. "I thought you'd be delivering papers."

"I'm always done before lunch," she explained. "So I thought I'd lend Nick a hand. Is that okay?"

"You can help out anytime you like," he said. "Maybe you can mention to that sister of yours what a nice fella I am."

"Deal," said Penny.

"Swell," said Uncle Spiro, and then he looked around. "Where's Ace?"

We told him about how Ace's ma had gotten him a job working for Happy.

Uncle Spiro busted out laughing. "I don't know who I feel more sorry for—Ace, because he has to work for Happy? Or Happy, because he has to put up with Ace." He wiped his eyes. "Let's get these cups into the freezer chest, or our frozen custard will be custard soup."

So we loaded up the cart and stepped back to admire Uncle Spiro's very own custard cart. He couldn't help smiling, and I couldn't blame him.

"I hope Athena found someone to work the cart," he said. "I really ought to get back to the shop."

"She promised that someone would be at Monkey Island at noon," I told him.

He checked his watch. "Five minutes. Let's go."

We wheeled the cart through the zoo to the shady patch of grass between Frosty's den and Monkey Island, and Sparky's Frozen Custard Cart was officially open for business.

There was Happy Harold's cart, right outside the main entrance of the zoo. Just like Ace had said, it was within spitting distance of Monkey Island.

And there was Ace, in a white shirt and black bow tie, with his soda-jerk hat slipping off his head. Pete was there, as ugly as ever. Apparently, he'd been roped into manning Happy's cart too. Ace spotted us and waved. I couldn't tell if he was saying hello or asking to be rescued.

And there was Happy, hollering at Ace and Pete about something. He must have caught sight of us out of the corner of his eye, because he suddenly stopped hollering and sneered in our direction.

Penny and I waved back.

"Poor Ace," said Penny, still waving. "Being stuck with Happy and Pete."

"I bet he wishes he'd kept that paper route after all," I said.

"Did Pete flunk a grade or something?" said Penny, squinting over to where Pete was chasing Ace around the other custard cart. "He's twice the size of everybody else in your grade."

"He's been bigger than the teacher since fourth grade," I said. "We've been in the same class since second grade. I remember because that's when he first beat me up."

"Where was he before then?" asked Penny.

I shrugged. "I don't remember him before then."

But I wasn't dumb enough to ask Pete to his face if he'd flunked a grade. If I really wanted to know, I'd have to find out some other way.

Just then, Some Other Way came sashaying toward us.

"Helloooo! Oh, helloooo!"

Uncle Spiro cringed without looking up. "Is that who I think it is?"

"Yep," I said as she wobbled up the path in high-heeled shoes. "Sophie Costas."

You might remember Sophie. Pete's big sister. "Maybe she's here to see Pete," I said, but no such luck. She was making a beeline for us.

Uncle Spiro took a deep breath and turned around to face the music. "Hullo, Sophie. How are you."

"Spiro, hello! Why, I'm just fine, thanks!" She gave the custard cart a once-over. "Isn't this adorable!"

"Want some custard?" said Uncle Spiro. "You can be our first customer."

"Gosh, no," fluttered Sophie. "I'm watching my figure." She batted her eyelids and smoothed her dress, which was a little on the fancy side for walking around the zoo, if you ask me. And she was twirling some crazy parasol over her head.

"Hiya, Sophie," I said.

She blinked at me and Penny like we'd appeared out of nowhere. "Oh, hello, Nicky. Hello, uh . . ."

"Penny," said Penny. She pushed back her hair, which was starting to pop loose from her braids. Then she said to Uncle Spiro, "Can I be your first customer?"

"Sure thing!" said Uncle Spiro, but before he could open the freezer chest, Sophie barged in.

"You might as well show me how it's done," she sang.

"How what's done?" I asked her.

"Serving frozen custard, of course!" She twirled her parasol.

Uncle Spiro's face went pale. "Did Athena send you?"

Sophie batted her lashes again. "I'm always willing to help a friend."

Penny nudged me and whispered, "What's going on?"

I told her how Ma had told Uncle Spiro she knew

someone from church who could help out, since the kid named Billy slipped on the ice.

"Ice? In June?" asked Penny.

"It's a long story," I told her. "Anyway, it looks like Sophie Costas is the person from church that Ma was talking about."

Uncle Spiro sighed and handed Sophie a blue apron. Sophie tried handing Spiro her parasol so she could put on the apron, but he wouldn't touch that thing. In the meantime, a line of people was forming behind Penny, who was still waiting for her custard.

Somehow Sophie managed to get the apron on. She twirled her parasol, even though there was plenty of shade from the big umbrella attached to the cart.

"This side of the freezer chest has chocolate," explained Uncle Spiro to Sophie, "and this side has vanilla. Ten cents a cup. The cash box is here. Don't let it out of your sight."

Sophie sidled up to Uncle Spiro. "It's going to be so much fun working together," she said.

"Together?" squeaked Uncle Spiro. "Sorry, Sophie, but I gotta get back to the shop. You let Nick here know if there's anything you need." And he escaped as quick as he could, leaving Sophie standing there with her mouth hanging open.

Penny stepped up and cleared her throat. "Chocolate, please."

CHAPTER

20

SOPHIE COSTAS LASTED ABOUT FIVE MINUTES. SHE
spent most of that time trying to serve custard with one
hand while she held that crazy parasol in her other hand,
and muttering about how this wasn't what she'd bargained
for. Then some little kid started bawling when she gave him
chocolate instead of vanilla, and that was it for Sophie. She
pulled off the apron, threw it onto the ground, and stomped
away as fast as she could in her high-heeled shoes.

"Bye, Sophie!" I hollered after her. To be honest, I was
disappointed that she was leaving already. I hadn't had a
chance to ask her if Pete had flunked a grade.

"Now what do we do?" said Penny as we watched
Sophie scurry off. "The line is getting pretty long."

She was right. It looked like I'd have to be in charge after all, at least for a little while. I picked up the apron from the grass and put it on.

Penny ran to Sparky's to tell Uncle Spiro that Sophie'd gone AWOL, while I held the fort at the custard cart, handing out cups and collecting money. In case anyone saw Happy Harold's cart and thought about going over there instead, I called out, "Step right up and get your custard! Sparky's frozen custard, the best in town! Only ten cents a cup!"

That's when I heard a voice floating over from the direction of the other custard cart.

"Happy's frozen custard!" hollered Pete. "Get your Happy Harold's custard, a tradition since 1942! Only *nine* cents a cup!" He looked in my direction with an evil grin. Happy was nowhere to be seen.

A bunch of people drifted away from my line and oozed toward Happy's. All so they could each save a penny. The nerve of that Pete.

I tried to ignore him as I served up custard. Then a bunch of little kids came whirling past and knocked into my cart, sending the napkin dispenser and the little wooden spoons flying all over the place.

"Hey, you kids!" I hollered after them as they ran toward Monkey Island.

But I couldn't pick up the napkins and spoons, because

people were still standing there, asking for custard. And I had to keep an eye on the cash box, because if something happened to that, I'd really be in hot water. All of a sudden it occurred to me: Being in charge was not all it was cracked up to be.

"Hey, kid," said the next fella in line. "Gimme six cups of vanilla and one cup of chocolate."

"You bet!" I said. I dug out the custard cups and stacked them on top of the cart. "That'll be seventy cents."

The fella looked at me. "Seventy cents?" He jutted his chin in the direction of Happy's cart. "That custard over there is only nine cents a cup. What gives?"

I didn't know what to say. I didn't know what to do.

The fella with the chin knew what to do. He turned around to leave, without his seven cups of custard.

"Okay!" I blurted. "Nine cents a cup! That'll be . . ."

"Sixty-three cents," said the chin fella, like he'd just made the deal of the century. "Got any napkins? Or spoons? What kind of outfit is this?"

That Pete was gonna hear an earful from me, if I ever got a chance to escape from Sparky's Frozen Custard Cart.

Somehow I managed to survive until Penny got back from the shop.

"What'd Uncle Spiro say about Sophie quitting?" I asked her.

She caught her breath and brushed the hair out of her

face. "Do you want to hear the word-for-word version, or the short version without the swear words?"

My face got hot. "The short version."

"He'll send help as soon as he can find someone. He's making some phone calls. What happened here?" She crouched down to gather up the spilled spoons and napkins.

"Long story," I said. And then I told her how Pete had lowered the price of his custard to nine cents.

"Can he do that?" said Penny.

"I dunno, but he did," I said. "And I started losing customers, so now I'm charging nine cents too."

"What?" said Penny. She glared over toward the other custard cart. "That Pete sure has a lot of nerve!"

"No kidding," I said. "Uncle Spiro's gonna kill me."

Penny marched over toward Happy's cart, fuming. I was glad that Penny was going to stick up for me, but I was also embarrassed that I couldn't do it for myself. But I didn't have much choice. I couldn't leave Sparky's cart.

I strained to hear what Penny was gonna say. But instead of walking up to the cart to holler at Pete, she went to the end of the line . . . and stood there, quietly waiting her turn. She turned toward me, nodded, and gave the thumbs-up.

What was she doing?

Pretty soon it was her turn in line. Ace bounced up, happy to see a friendly face. Pete loomed over Penny across the custard cart. Then he reached into the cart and handed

Penny a cup of custard, and Penny put something into Pete's hand. A dime, I guessed. Pete put something into her hand. A penny. Then she turned away, slurping her cup of Happy Harold's custard.

And I'd thought Penny was on my side.

I turned back to serve my next customer, trying to block out the sight of one of my best pals turning traitor.

Then, from behind me, I heard someone say, "*Blech!* You call this custard? This is awful!"

I turned around, and there was Penny, right next to Happy's custard cart, making the ugliest face I'd ever seen. "I can't believe I wasted nine cents on this stuff! I sure wish I'd gone to Sparky's for custard!"

And then something magical happened: The line of people waiting for Happy's custard kind of dissolved, and they all came drifting over toward me.

Good ol' Penny. I never should've doubted her.

CHAPTER

21

NOW THERE WAS A REALLY LONG LINE OF PEOPLE waiting for custard at Sparky's cart and pretty much no one at Happy's.

I got to work handing out custard and collecting money as quick as I could. "Get your Sparky's custard!" I hollered. "Ten cents a cup! Everybody knows it's the best in town!"

Pete glared over and shook his fist at me. But he couldn't come over and clobber me, because that would leave Ace in charge of Happy Harold's cart, and even Pete knew better than to do that.

Penny came scurrying back. "How'd I do?" she said.

"That was swell!" I told her. I looked at the cup of Happy's custard in her hand. "What're you gonna do with that?"

She looked around. "Where's the trash barrel?"

"Over there on the other side of the path," I told her, pointing toward Monkey Island.

She crossed the path and lifted the cup to toss it into the trash barrel. But then she stopped, without dropping it. She looked toward Monkey Island. She tilted her head. Then she stepped closer and peeked over the fence that surrounded the moat, with the cup still in her hand.

She scurried back toward me.

"What happened?" I asked. "How come you didn't throw away the custard?"

"It's Maxene!" she said. "She's swimming in the moat again, looking at me!"

"How do you know it's Maxene?" I said. "There's a million monkeys over there, and they all look alike."

"It's her, all right," said Penny. "I'd know those eyebrows anywhere. And I think she wants custard! What should I do?"

"If it's chocolate, don't bother," I said, remembering how Ace almost got beaned when Maxene tossed my cone back over the fence the other day.

"It's vanilla."

I shrugged and pointed to a sign on the fence that said PLEASE DON'T FEED THE ANIMALS. But no one pays attention to those signs, and like I said earlier, the zookeepers have a hard time keeping up. That's how everyone knows that the elephant loves peanuts and Frosty loves marshmallows.

Right now, I craned my neck to try and see Maxene, but the surface of the moat was below the bottom of the fence. And my line of customers was really long, and I was darned if I'd let any of them drift back to Happy's cart. I had to stay put and keep serving up custard.

I knew I should tell Penny to toss the custard cup in the trash barrel. But part of me really wanted to know what Maxene would do this time.

Penny must've been thinking the same thing, because she sidled over to the fence surrounding Monkey Island, waited until no one was looking, and then dropped the cup of custard over the fence.

I still couldn't see anything, but I heard the splash. And then Penny turned and gave me a thumbs-up.

"How about that?" I said as she came scurrying back to the cart. "Maxene likes vanilla."

Just then, I heard someone calling my name.

"Oh, Nicky!"

I knew that voice. It belonged to the only person in the world who's allowed to call me Nicky in public.

Penny and I turned around. Here she came up the path, wearing sunglasses and a big silk scarf over her head, waving at us. It was her favorite scarf—the one with a map of Greece on it, that her cousin sent her one Christmas.

"Ma! What are you doing here? Why are you wearing a disguise?"

"Disguise?" she said, adjusting the scarf. "I wear this just in case."

"In case of what?"

She shot a glance over her sunglasses. "In case the monkeys. I don't want them in my hair."

"Aw, gee, Ma," I told her. "The monkeys aren't gonna get out."

She raised an eyebrow at me. Then she waved at the custard cart. "You need help, *neh*?"

I looked down the long line of people still waiting for custard. "How did you know?"

"*Hmph!*" said Ma, taking off her gloves. "The doorbell rings, and there is Sophia Costas, crying! She says Spiro was rude to her. Can you believe? Spiro? And then, Spiro calls on the telephone, says that Sophia quit! But he can't leave the shop, and he needs someone else at the zoo right away!" She dropped her gloves into her pocketbook, snapped it shut, and held out a hand. "Apron."

I took it off and handed it over. Then she stepped behind the cart and clapped her hands. "Who wants frozen custard?" she called. "Vanilla? Choc-o-late? Ten cents, free spoon! Who's next?"

The two little kids at the front of the line stopped shoving each other long enough to both holler, "Chocolate!"

and then they went back to their shoving match.

"Stop that right now!" said Ma. "You want ice-a cream? Be nice boys!"

The two kids froze. They blinked up at Ma and gulped. The bigger kid stood up straight, held out a quarter, and squeaked, "Two chocolates. Please. Ma'am."

Ma's stern face melted into a sweet smile. "Very nice! Good boy." She plopped the quarter into the cash box and gave the kid a nickel, along with two cups of custard. Then, before the kid knew what was happening, Ma reached across the cart and pinched him on the cheek.

I've been getting my cheeks pinched for twelve years. It doesn't hurt or anything. But it *is* embarrassing. All I could think now was, Better you than me, kid.

Next in line was a little girl in a pink dress and crumpled ankle socks, with a head full of braids, half hiding behind her mother.

"A cup of vanilla, please," said the mother.

Ma cooed to the little girl. "You like custard, *koukla mou*? You know what that means? It means 'my little doll.' Because you are the most beautiful little girl in the whole world!"

At which point the girl's mother beamed, the little girl stepped out into the open, and Ma swooped down and pinched her on the cheek.

CHAPTER 22

THAT'S HOW MA TOOK OVER SPARKY'S FROZEN Custard Cart at the zoo. She spent the whole afternoon scolding, sweet-talking, and pinching cheeks—and selling custard like hotcakes. Me and Penny had to run back to the shop twice for more inventory. During our second trip through the zoo with our fresh supply, I overheard people saying that the best place to get a snack was at the custard cart across from Monkey Island. Little kids were even bragging about getting their cheeks pinched by the lady with the map on her head.

As Penny and I loaded Sparky's cart with fresh cups of custard, I peeked over toward Happy Harold's cart. "Hey, look," I told Penny. "It's the big boss."

There was grumpy ol' Happy himself, giving Ace and Pete an earful about something.

"Poor Ace," said Penny. "He looks miserable."

She was right. Even from here I could see Ace was looking a little green around the gills. If Happy wasn't careful, he was gonna end up with another pair of ruined shoes.

"Pete doesn't look so hot either." I never thought I'd say this about my worst enemy, but for once I almost felt sorry for him.

"Can you hear what Happy's saying?" said Penny.

"Nope."

"Should we go over there and find out?"

"Not a chance," I told her. "Happy'll start hollering at us next."

Now Pete was pointing in our direction.

Happy stopped talking. He looked this way and gave us the stink-eye.

"I bet he's hollering at Pete for lowering their price to nine cents a cup," Penny guessed.

"Or maybe he's sore because our line of customers is twice as long as his." I waved. "Hiya, Happy! How's it going?"

Ace waved back. Happy scowled even harder.

"Nicky!" said Ma, nudging me. "Take over for five minutes, *neh*? I need to powder my nose." She slipped the apron over her head and handed it to me.

"So do I," said Penny, and together they headed toward the pavilion, and the bathrooms.

I turned to the little kid who was next in line. "What'll it be?"

He pouted. "Where's the funny lady going?"

"To powder her nose."

"Why?"

I didn't think Ma would want me telling some goofy little kid that she had to go to the bathroom. So I said, "She'll be back in a few minutes."

The kid looked at the dime in his hand. He turned around and scanned the line of people behind him. He put the dime in his pocket. "I'll come back later." And he actually walked all the way to the back of the line. It was the first time I'd ever seen a kid wait in line for custard twice, on purpose. The line snaked around Monkey Island, so at least he had something to watch while he waited. I guess he figured it was worth it, if he'd get to see the funny lady for himself.

"Hey, kid! You working here or what?"

I looked up. It was the fella with the chin from earlier who'd badgered me into selling him seven cups of custard for nine cents apiece. This time he was holding a kid by the hand, and the kid was eating a blob of cotton candy. Most of it was stuck on his face.

"The price has gone back up," I told the chin fella. "Ten cents a cup."

He narrowed his eyes at me. The sticky kid whined about wanting custard *now*. "Fine," said the chin fella. "Gimme one vanilla and one strawberry."

I blinked at him. "We don't have strawberry. It's chocolate or vanilla."

He looked at me like I'd just told him that custard was made by monkeys. "What d'ya mean, no strawberry?"

What could I say? "Sorry. Nobody sells strawberry custard."

He jutted his chin in the direction of Happy's cart. "That fella does."

I turned around, and sure enough, there was grumpy ol' Happy, tacking a big sign onto his cart that said NOW SERVING STRAWBERRY CUSTARD!

"How about it?" said the chin fella. "You got strawberry or not?"

"No!"

"Then I'm goin' over there. C'mon, Dewey." And he pulled his sticky, whiny kid after him.

The news traveled fast. People murmured and muttered, and then a whole bunch of them drifted away from Sparky's line and joined the line in front of Happy's cart. For strawberry custard.

That left two or three people waiting for Sparky's custard, looking like they were there only because they felt sorry for me. I served them, and then there was nobody except the kid who'd gone to the end of the line a few minutes ago.

"The funny lady's not back yet?" he said. "Her nose didn't look that big."

"I dunno, kid," I sighed. "Want some custard?"

He looked down at the dime in his hand. He looked over toward Happy's cart. "No thanks," he said, pocketing his dime.

And he wandered over to stand in line again—this time to wait for strawberry custard.

CHAPTER

23

THE NEXT MORNING, WE ALL MET UP AT THE SHOP to lick our wounds.

Ace and I were getting settled when Penny came busting in. "Strawberry! Where'd that come from?" She tossed her empty newspaper sack onto a stool.

"Don't ask me," said Ace. "It was nothing but chocolate and vanilla when I got there. And then, out of nowhere, Happy shows up with this whole supply of strawberry."

"On the very same day Sparky's opens for business at the zoo?" I said. "I'll bet he did it to spite us."

"It's not spite," said Uncle Spiro as he scooped a fresh batch of custard into wax-paper cups. "It's just business. You gotta stay a step ahead of the competition." He chuckled. "To be honest, I wish I'd thought of it."

Ace helped himself to a cup of chocolate. "Boy, did Happy fume when he saw your cart out there! He wasn't expecting you till the weekend."

"We saw him hollering at you and Pete," I said. "Jeepers. It wasn't your fault we opened early."

Ace pulled the top off his custard cup and licked it clean. "Happy said that if Sparky can use a secret ingredient, it was time for him to deploy *his* secret weapon."

Uncle Spiro laughed out loud.

"What's so funny?" I said. "How come you're not taking this seriously?"

"I am," said Spiro. "I just think it's funny that Happy still thinks I'm using a secret ingredient."

"Well, aren't you?" said Ace. He leaned closer and whispered, "You know—the whiskey?" He glanced around to make sure no one else had heard, even though the shop was still closed.

Penny and I looked at Uncle Spiro, but no one said a thing. We never did tell Ace that whiskey wasn't actually an ingredient in Sparky's custard.

Uncle Spiro coughed. "Oh, that? I, uh . . . discontinued it. Not good for the kids, you know."

Ace bought that story, I guess, because he settled back down with his custard. "Too bad," he said. "Secret-ingredient custard sounds swell."

Penny laughed. "That could be *our* third flavor."

And then I had a stroke of genius.

"That's it!" I said. "Why can't we have our own third flavor? Something even better than strawberry?"

"There's nothing better than strawberry," said Ace.

I gave him a shove. "Whose side are you on, anyway?"

"He does work for Happy," said Penny.

Uncle Spiro thought about it. "Our own third flavor? Why not? We could mix something tasty into the vanilla."

"Like nuts," said Penny. "Or blueberries."

"Or chocolate chips," said Ace.

But I had the best idea. "Chopped-up marshmallows."

"Marshmallows?" said Uncle Spiro. He sat up straight. "I like it!"

And then I got an even better idea. "We could call it Frosty Freeze."

"Right," said Ace. "Because Frosty loves marshmallows!"

"It's perfect," said Uncle Spiro. "Ever since Frosty escaped, that's all anyone can talk about." He gazed at the ceiling, reading an imaginary banner. "'Get your Sparky's custard! Vanilla! Chocolate! And our newest flavor: Frosty Freeze!'"

Penny's eyes got wide. "I'd stand in a very long line for Frosty Freeze custard," she said.

"I'd even *pay* for Frosty Freeze custard," said Ace.

"Hold on, fellas," I said. "We could still add a secret ingredient."

Uncle Spiro rubbed his hands together. "I like that, too! Give folks even more to talk about. All we need is the right ingredient. Something that tastes delicious in custard but isn't obvious."

"Like whiskey!" said Ace.

We all looked at him.

His ears turned red. "But not whiskey," he squeaked. "That'd be dumb."

I turned back to Uncle Spiro. "You mean an ingredient that's *in* the food, and it makes the food taste better, but you can't taste the actual ingredient?"

"Right."

"I might know just the thing," I said. "I need to talk to Ma."

"You do that," said Uncle Spiro. He raised a cup of custard in a toast. "It's official, fellas. Operation Frosty Freeze is underway."

CHAPTER

24

THAT AFTERNOON, WHEN ME AND MA WERE IN between customers at the zoo cart, I told her my idea.

"Cinnamon-flavored custard?" she said. "With marshmallows?"

"Shh," I said. "It's a secret. Do you think it would taste good?"

Ma scowled over toward Happy's cart, where Pete was serving up cups of strawberry as fast as he could. She was still sore about Happy skirting the rules. "I think it would taste delicious."

That night, we brought home some cups of vanilla and started experimenting. First, Ma boiled a cinnamon stick in a pan of water. Once it was cool, we mixed a little of the liquid into a cup of custard. Then she chopped up some marshmallows and stirred those in too.

"We must wait maybe an hour," explained Ma, putting it into the freezer. "For it to freeze up again, *neh*? Let's try something else while we wait. An old family recipe."

"For frozen custard?"

"Why not?" She turned on the flame under the pan of cinnamon liquid to warm it up again. Then she opened a cupboard and pulled out a small jar. "Let's add this," she said, unscrewing the lid and shaking out a few dark brown nuggets with star-shaped ends. They looked like tiny, dried flowers in her hand. The jar smelled spicy, like cinnamon but different.

"What are they?" I asked her.

"Cloves," said Ma. She plopped two of the nuggets into the pot of warm cinnamon water. Once that was cooled down, she fished out the cloves and mixed the syrup into a second cup of custard. She mixed in some more marshmallows and stuck the whole thing into the freezer. Then, to pass the time, we sat down and listened to an episode of *The Abbott and Costello Show* on the radio.

Finally it was tasting time. We each spooned a bit from the first cup—the one with only the cinnamon flavor and marshmallows.

I licked my spoon. "It's good, but it's not exactly secret. It definitely tastes like cinnamon."

"Hm," said Ma, examining her own spoonful. "You are right. Not secret enough. Let's try the other recipe."

We dug into sample number two.

"Yum!" I said. "It looks like plain ol' vanilla, but it tastes like . . . what does it taste like?"

"It tastes like the old country," said Ma with a happy sigh. "Like home. Many of the old Greek recipes, they use a bit of cinnamon and clove together. And the marshmallows taste . . . American." She licked her spoon clean. "I think this one is delicious *and* secret."

She was right. This was getting exciting. "Let's find out how secret," I told her. "We need a guinea pig to taste it."

Ma looked offended. "You are going to feed my recipe to a pig?"

"No, Ma. A guinea pig. Someone who tastes something without knowing what they're tasting."

"Ah," said Ma, relaxing. "Your father!"

We found him in the front room, reading the newspaper.

"Hiya, Pop," I said. "We need an opinion."

"That's right," said Ma, taking the newspaper out of his hands. "Right now, you must be a pig."

Pop frowned at that, but he brightened up when he saw that he only had to taste some frozen custard. He took a bite.

"Mmm," he said. "Marshmallows!" Then he licked his lips. "What else do I taste? This is not the same vanilla I usually eat."

"You are supposed to guess," said Ma, folding her arms.

Pop examined his spoonful. "It looks like Spiro's vanilla, but I taste something else. I cannot be sure. . . ." He took another bite. He smiled, shrugged, and kept eating.

I gave Ma a thumbs-up. "So far, so good."

She looked around. "Who else can be a pig for us?"

"How about Ace?" I ran next door to get him, and for good measure I grabbed his little sister, too. Ma sat them down at the kitchen table and gave them each a spoonful of the second custard.

"What it tastes like to you?" she asked, tapping her foot.

"Marshmallows!" said Ace right away.

"What else?"

"It's yummy," said Ace's little sister. "It tastes . . . like apple pie without the apples."

"She's right," said Ace. He polished off his sample and held out his empty spoon. "Let me taste again."

Ma gave them both a second spoonful. They finished those, too, but still couldn't guess the flavor.

Ma and I looked at each other, and we both busted out grinning.

"I think we've found our recipe," I said.

Ace held up his empty spoon. "You mean this is Sparky's new third flavor? This is Frosty Freeze?"

"If Uncle Spiro gives the go-ahead," I said.

"No wonder you didn't tell us what's in it!" said Ace.

He leaned closer and whispered, "What's in it?"

I shook my head. "Nope. You work for the enemy, remember?"

"You have been very helpful," Ma told Ace and his little sister. She opened the back door. "Now go home."

A few minutes later, Uncle Spiro walked in. "What's for supper, Athena? I'm starving!"

"Custard first, then supper," said Ma, plunking the almost-empty cup in front of him.

His face lit up. "You're working on Operation Frosty Freeze already?"

"Sorry there's not much left," said Ma. "The pigs were tasting."

Uncle Spiro lifted an eyebrow, but he knew better than to ask Ma to explain. He took a bite. He scraped his spoon around the inside of the cup and licked it clean. Then he licked the cup.

"Do you like it?" I said. "Me and Ma invented it."

"I love it!" said Uncle Spiro. "What's in it, besides marshmallows?"

"It's a secret," I said.

"Fair enough," said Uncle Spiro. He reached out and shook my hand and then Ma's. "Congratulations, fellas. Operation Frosty Freeze is a go!"

CHAPTER
25

RAY: *Top* o' the morning, folks! It's your old pals Ray and Bob here on WTRJ radio, bringing you all the latest news, sports, and weather.

BOB: Let's get right to it! In baseball news, I see the Mudpuppies lost again. Twelve to nothing in ten innings.

RAY: Golly. That tenth inning must have been a doozy.

BOB: I'll say. That makes six straight losses for the Pups. But it doesn't mean you can't have fun down at the ballpark, folks!

RAY: That's right, Bob. I heard that before the game, team owner Joe Daggett himself put on a Pups uniform and pitched batting practice.

BOB: Maybe he should've pitched the tenth inning.

RAY: In local news, the city zoo's resident polar bear had his annual dental checkup yesterday.

BOB: You mean Frosty? How'd that go, Ray? And how the heck did he fit in the dentist's chair?

RAY: Well, Bob, there's no need for a chair because the dentist comes to him. It seems that Frosty has some cavities that'll need filling.

BOB: A few too many marshmallows, I'm guessing.

RAY: Those "Don't Feed the Animals" signs might need to be bigger, don't you think?

BOB: It sure is hard to resist when Frosty sits up on his hind legs to beg for marshmallows.

RAY: Sounds like you've tossed one or two marshmallows Frosty's way yourself there, Bob.

BOB: Shh! Don't tell the zookeepers, ha ha.

RAY: *Ahem.* Say, remember a couple of weeks ago, when Frosty decided to take an early-morning stroll through the neighborhood?

BOB: How could I forget? I think there's a milkman who'd like to forget, though.

RAY: Poor fella. Well, some new information has come to light. It seems that on the morning in question, a stick was found, stuck in Frosty's door.

BOB: A stuck stick? Who would stick a stick in Frosty's door?

RAY: That's the crux, isn't it, Bob?

BOB: Crux? But you just said it was a stick.

RAY: It *was* a stick, Bob. "Crux" means "the most important part of an issue."

BOB: If you ask me, I'd say that stick was pretty important. That stuck stick let loose a half-ton polar bear, for heaven's sake.

RAY: Who would stick a stick in Frosty's door, Bob? I don't think Frosty has the dexterity to do it himself.

BOB: Dex—what? You're wearing me out here, Ray.

RAY: Dexterity. It means "having nimble fingers."

BOB: Oh. Say, you know who has nimble fingers? Monkeys!

RAY: Are you saying that a monkey jimmied Frosty's door open, Bob? Wouldn't it more likely be a human?

BOB: What kind of human would be foolish enough to let a polar bear out of his cage, Ray? That's just asking for trouble. A monkey, though . . . he wouldn't know any better.

RAY: Speaking of monkeys, today's a great day to head on down to the zoo, folks. We're expecting sunny skies and a high of seventy-five. So get out there and enjoy it if you can, because tomorrow looks like rain.

BOB: I'll be heading to the zoo myself, Ray. I hear they're serving a swell new flavor at Sparky's custard cart. It's called Frosty Freeze.

RAY: Sounds delicious! I think I'll mosey on down to the zoo sometime and give Frosty Freeze a try.

BOB: Good idea. And while you're there, take a look at those monkeys and their dex . . . their nimble fingers!

✳ ✳ ✳

Even before those two fellas talked about it on the radio, Frosty Freeze custard was a hit. Every night, Ma cooked up a batch of cinnamon-and-clove syrup and chopped up a pile of marshmallows. Early every morning, Uncle Spiro took it all to the shop and mixed it into a fresh batch of vanilla custard. And every day before noon, I loaded the cups into the freezer chest and wheeled it down to the zoo in my Radio Flyer wagon.

It sold like gangbusters. And now the whole city knew about it, thanks to Ray and Bob.

"Did you hear the radio?" I called as I busted into the shop that morning.

"Yep!" said Uncle Spiro. "Pretty swell!" He was busy packing the day's batch of custard.

"Maybe we should crank up production," I told him. "Skip selling vanilla for a while, and make more Frosty Freeze."

"Nope." He kept on scooping, casual as could be.

I didn't get it. "But we were on the radio! You're gonna have a line of customers from here to Chicago this afternoon!"

"I sure as heck hope so," he said.

I still didn't get it. "You don't want to disappoint folks, do you? We're gonna run out for sure!"

Uncle Spiro set down his scooper. "Do you know about supply and demand, Nick?"

Sounded like school stuff. "No."

"I can't *supply* enough Frosty Freeze to keep up with *demand*, right?"

"Right."

"What do you think would happen if I did increase the supply? If folks could have as much Frosty Freeze as they wanted, whenever they wanted it?"

That was easy. "You'd sell more custard. You'd make a ton of money. You'd—"

He shook his head. "Frosty Freeze wouldn't be so special anymore. Eventually, folks would get tired of it. They might even wander over to Happy's for a cup of strawberry."

That would not be good. "So you *want* to run out of Frosty Freeze?"

"Now you got it, Nick." He shook a finger at me and winked. "Always leave 'em wanting more."

CHAPTER

26

I LEFT THE CUSTARD SHOP AND WANDERED OVER to Penny's house to see if she was home from her paper route.

Sure enough, she was sitting on her front porch steps, eating a donut. "Want one?" she said. "My mom made 'em special. My sister Josie's coming home from Kenosha."

I sat down and took a donut. It was still warm. "Already? I was hoping we could go see her pitch a game."

Penny shook her head. "She's out for the season, isn't that awful? Broke the pinky of her pitching hand." Penny popped the last of her donut into her mouth and brushed the sugar off her fingers. As usual, not a crumb anywhere.

"That's too bad," I said. "What happened? Sharp line drive back to the mound?"

"Not exactly. She dropped her lipstick in the locker room, and when she reached down to pick it up, another player accidentally stepped on her hand."

"Holy smokes," I said.

"I know," said Penny. But then she perked up. "My dad's on his way to get her right now. Today's his day off."

"So that's why his motorcycle is still here." I pointed toward that shiny police-department Harley parked at the curb.

Penny nodded. "They should be home by lunchtime."

"Hiya, fellas!" Here came Ace up the sidewalk. I tell ya, that kid can sniff out hot donuts from two blocks away. "Did you hear?" he said. "They talked about Frosty on the radio. And Frosty Freeze, too!" He licked his lips. "What's that, Penny? Donuts?"

"Fresh out of the fryer," she said, offering the plate. "What did they say on the radio?"

"Frosty has cavities," said Ace, plopping down and helping himself to a donut. "Poor ol' Frosty. I hate going to the dentist. Got anything to wash this down with?"

"Mom!" hollered Penny through the screen door. "Can we have sodas?"

"That's not the best part," I said. "They found a stick in Frosty's door!"

"Oh, that," said Penny, braiding up her cloud of hair. "It was actually a small tree branch."

Me and Ace both stopped with donuts halfway to our mouths.

"They didn't say that on the radio," said Ace.

She gave a casual shrug. "It's in the official police report."

Behind us, the screen door opened, and Penny's ma handed over three bottles of soda. Ace grabbed grape, I took cream, and Penny was stuck with lime. So I traded with her because I'm a gentleman.

"Bring the empties inside when you're done," said Penny's ma. "Your father will want to return them for the deposit."

We all promised, and waited politely for her to go back inside.

"Tell us about the police report!" I said after Penny's ma was gone.

Penny lowered her voice. "Last night I heard my dad talking on the phone with one of his buddies down at the station. According to the police report, a small branch was found wedged in Frosty's doorway to keep it from latching shut." She brushed invisible crumbs off her knee. "And all its bark had been stripped off."

Me and Ace tried to act like we weren't impressed, but who were we kidding? I sat there for a minute, letting the information soak in. Ace took another donut.

Finally I said, "Stripped bark? Is that a clue?"

Penny shrugged. "But they're pretty sure that someone put the stick there on purpose."

Ace gave a low whistle. "Who'd be nasty enough to let a polar bear out on purpose?"

I took a guess. "Happy Harold?"

Penny and Ace both looked at me like I'd lost my marbles.

But the more I thought about it, the more it made sense.

"Remember what South Side Lenny said that day when he came into Sparky's shop? He said that Happy has a real sore spot for Mr. Stankey, because Mr. Stankey won't let him open a second custard cart at the zoo."

"I remember," said Ace. "So?"

"So, maybe Happy wanted to get even with Mr. Stankey."

"By letting loose a polar bear?" said Penny.

"Maybe Happy didn't expect Frosty to actually escape," I said, thinking out loud. "Maybe he only wanted someone to find the door unlatched."

"I'm not sure . . . ," said Penny.

"Think about it," I said. "Mr. Stankey goes around every night at closing time to make sure everything's locked up, right? Maybe that night, Happy followed him and jammed the stick in Frosty's door when Mr. Stankey wasn't looking, figuring that in the morning, someone would discover the unlatched door, and BAM! Mr. Stankey's in big trouble. Fired, even."

Ace's eyes got big. "Maybe Happy tipped off the news-papers, too. To make sure people found out about it."

We all sat on the top step of Penny's front porch, feeling the weight of the world in our stomachs. Or maybe it was the weight of donuts and soda.

"I gotta go," said Ace after a minute. "If I'm late at Happy's cart, he'll tell my ma." And he took off without finishing his grape soda, which proved one thing: Ace was plenty scared of Happy, but he was even more scared of his ma.

M E AND PENNY CAUGHT UP WITH ACE AND WALKED with him to the zoo. When we got there, one of the zookeepers was hanging a poster. It said:

INDEPENDENCE DAY AT THE ZOO
Sunday, July 4th
Presentation of colors

KIDZ KAZOO PARADE
Bring your kazoo!

BAND SHELL CONCERT
Featuring the Riverwest High School Orchestra

FIREWORKS

At dusk

All events free and open to the public

COME ONE! COME ALL!

Show your patriotic spirit!

"A Fourth of July party!" said Penny. "Right here at the zoo?"

"It's the best day of the whole summer," I said, because Penny was still pretty new in town. "There's big crowds, and flags and streamers, and music over the loudspeakers."

"And hot dogs," said Ace. "Don't forget about the hot dogs."

Me and Penny left Ace at Happy's cart, and then we walked another two blocks to Sparky's Custard Shop.

"Hiya, fellas!" said Uncle Spiro, who was unlocking the front door. "Today's supply of custard is all packed and ready to go." He flipped his sign from CLOSED to OPEN.

"I'll walk back to the zoo with you, Nick," said Penny. "But then I'm going home to see Josie."

"Josie?" said Uncle Spiro, perking up. "Your big sister's home from Kenosha?"

Penny nodded and explained the whole lipstick-and-broken-finger situation.

"Gee, that's too bad," said Spiro, but he had a big, goofy grin on his face.

Me and Penny went to the back room for the day's supply of custard. We lifted the full freezer chest onto the Radio Flyer, and then we wheeled it around the counter and toward the front door.

Just then, the door jingled open and in walked two fellas, about sixteen or seventeen years old. Uncle Spiro's first customers of the day.

"Hey! Sparky!" said one of the kids, swaggering across the room. "Gimme a double scoop of Frosty Freeze. In a cone. And make it snappy." He tossed a dime onto the counter and leaned on an elbow. A pack of cigarettes was rolled up in the sleeve of his grubby T-shirt.

"Same here," said the second kid, with another clank of coins.

"All the Frosty Freeze is already packed for the zoo," said Uncle Spiro, nodding toward the Radio Flyer wagon and the freezer chest. "How about a couple of cups? Same price."

The two kids looked at the wagon and then back to Spiro.

"But we don't want our custard in cups, Sparky," said the first kid, flexing his muscles. "We want it in cones. So, why don't you just reach into that freezer chest and start scooping?"

I knew for a fact that if they'd asked nicely, Uncle Spiro would've happily obliged these fellas.

But they hadn't asked nicely.

Spiro picked up a rag and started wiping the counter, careful not to touch the coins. "Sorry, fellas. If you want a cone, I got vanilla and chocolate."

The second kid leaned over the counter. "We don't want vanilla or chocolate. We want Frosty Freeze."

Uncle Spiro leaned over the counter too, until he was nose to nose with the kid. "Then I guess you'll have to have it in a cup."

"Come on, Penny," I said, pushing the door open. I figured these two tough guys couldn't argue if what they wanted was off the premises.

"Hey!" said the first kid. "Where do you think you're going?"

I tried once more to push past him.

"Nick," said Uncle Spiro without taking his eyes off the kid. "Stay where you are." He plucked the coins from the counter and held them out. "And you two can take these when you leave, which is now."

For a second, the two kids seemed to think about making more trouble. But then Uncle Spiro rolled up his sleeves and walked around from behind the counter, demonstrating that lots of time scooping frozen custard (not to mention a couple of years in the war) will give you real muscles, whereas a pack of cigarettes rolled up in the sleeve of your T-shirt makes you a real knucklehead.

The first kid snatched the coins out of Spiro's hand and stormed toward the door. "You think you're a big shot, Sparky? That little red wagon has to leave this shop sooner or later." And they stomped out the door and parked themselves on the sidewalk.

"Now what are we gonna do?" I squeaked. "Even if we go out the back, they'll see us. We need to get this custard to the zoo. It'll start melting. Customers will be waiting. Ma will wonder what happened to us. What if those two radio fellas show up? We can't disappoint the radio fellas!"

"I dunno, Nick," said Spiro. He sounded tired. I guess being tough can be pretty exhausting.

And then, out of the blue, Penny said, "Uncle Spiro, can I use your telephone?"

"Sure." He pointed to the phone hanging on the wall behind the counter.

Penny slipped behind the counter, picked up the receiver, and ran her finger around the dial a few times.

"Who's she calling?" said Uncle Spiro.

I shrugged.

Penny held the receiver to her ear for a few seconds, and then she said, "Hello, Mom? Is Daddy home from Kenosha yet? Good. Can I talk to him?"

"Ohhh," I said. "Now I get it."

"You do?" said Uncle Spiro.

"Yep. She's calling the police."

CHAPTER

28

AND THAT'S HOW ME AND PENNY GOT A POLICE escort from Sparky's Custard Shop all the way to the zoo.

Well, it was only Penny's dad on his day off, wearing civilian clothes under his leather jacket and police helmet, driving his Harley at two miles per hour, lights swirling and siren whooping, while we walked behind him for two blocks with a little red wagon full of frozen custard.

It was swell.

Let me tell you, that kind of thing will attract attention. When those two tough kids saw that police motorcycle roar up to Sparky's, they took off like they'd robbed a bank. And by the time we got to the zoo, a whole crowd of kids was following us, as if Penny's dad was the Pied Piper. The whole procession wound through the zoo, past Frosty's enclosure and Monkey Island, and along the path to Sparky's cart, where Ma stood waiting in her sunglasses and map-of-Greece scarf, tapping her foot.

She pulled at my elbow and shot a glance toward the policeman on his motorcycle. "What happens, Nicky? Did you do the jaywalking or something?"

"No, Ma! That's Penny's dad!"

Ma frowned at me, then at Penny's dad, and then at me again. "Why?"

"It's a long story," I told her as me and Penny hoisted the freezer chest out of the Radio Flyer and onto the custard cart.

"I'll see you later, Nick," said Penny. "I'm going home to see Josie!" And she hopped onto that Harley behind her dad, and they puttered away through the crowd. Lucky ol' Penny.

Ma nudged me back to reality. "We have customers already."

She was right. There was a line of people waiting for custard, and we hadn't even opened yet. I guess that's what happens when you're mentioned on the radio.

I couldn't help it. I looked over toward Happy's cart to see if he'd noticed.

He'd noticed, all right. It's hard to miss a big ol' police

motorcycle rumbling past. I could see Happy's snarl from here. Which meant that Ace and Pete were probably about to get an earful from their boss.

Sure enough, Happy turned around and laid into Pete. Then Pete turned around and laid into Ace. And poor ol' Ace had no one to holler at.

I turned my back on that disaster and set up the napkins and little wooden spoons on Sparky's cart. And I reminded Ma that the radio fellas might stop by.

"The ones who say '*Top* o' the morning,' *neh*?" she said. "I will be ready. What these two people look like?"

That was a good question. "I only know what they sound like."

Ma straightened her apron. "One of them is tall and skinny. The other one is short and fat. With a mustache."

"Really? How do you know that?"

She shrugged. "That's what they sound like to me."

I couldn't prove her wrong. "They might not show up together," I told her. "They might not show up at all."

"They will show up," said Ma, and if those radio fellas knew what was good for them, they'd better not disappoint my mother.

Ma started serving custard. Every time a likely fella stepped up, she squinted at him and barked, "Say '*Top* o' the morning!'"

"Top of the what?" said one confused customer.

"'Top o' the morning!'" said Ma. "It means 'Wake up.' Say it."

"Uh . . . top o' the morning?"

"No," said Ma, mentally crossing him off her list. She served him his custard and shooed him away so she could look out for the next fella.

After twenty minutes of interrogating every short, tall, fat, thin, and mustachioed man in line—in other words, every man in line—Ma heaved a sigh and stretched her back. "I'm getting too old to be nice to so many people," she muttered.

That's when I heard a loud voice coming from the direction of Happy's cart.

"Step right up, folks, and don't miss out! Get your strawberry custard before it's gone! Only a few cups left!"

Next, Happy pulled down his sign that had NOW SERVING STRAWBERRY CUSTARD! scribbled on it and then tacked it up again. The words NOW SERVING were crossed out, and he'd written GOING FAST!

Ma scowled when she saw that. "What Happy is doing now?"

I scowled too. "Looks like Happy's figured out supply and demand."

"What?" said Ma.

"Uncle Spiro told me about it. Always leave them wanting more."

Happy's plan seemed to be working. A few people scurried from Sparky's line over to Happy's.

I felt a nudge at my elbow again. "Nicky!" said Ma. "Look."

Two fellas dressed in shirts and ties were walking up the path toward us. One of them was tall and skinny. The other one was short and fat. With a mustache.

"*Top* o' the mornin' to ya, young lady!" boomed the tall one to Ma.

She shot me a satisfied look.

I don't know how she knows what she knows. But it makes a kid think twice before sneaking a dime or two out of her purse, that's for sure.

The short fella looked the cart up and down. "So this is Sparky's!"

Ma beamed. "Have some frozen custard. Homemade, with a very nice secret ingredient."

"Hey . . . ," said the kid who was next in line. "No skips!"

Ma turned to the kid and said, "Shh! Be good." She opened the freezer chest, pulled out two cups of Frosty Freeze, and handed them over to the radio fellas with a flourish. "Just for you, Mr. Ray. Mr. Bob. No charge."

"Isn't that neighborly of you!" boomed Ray. Or maybe it was Bob. They stepped into the shade of a nearby tree, pulled the cardboard lids off their cups, and dug in with their little wooden spoons.

"Ahem." It was the kid who was next in line, still looking a little peeved.

Ma blinked at him as if he'd materialized out of thin air. "What flavor?"

"The special," he said, eyeing her suspiciously, as if he didn't trust that he'd finally get his custard.

But Ma came through. She handed over a cup of Frosty Freeze and held up her hand. "No charge this time."

The kid's face lit up with a surprised smile. That's when Ma swooped down and pinched him on the cheek.

CHAPTER

29

WHEN RAY AND BOB THE RADIO FELLAS HAD finished their custard, they moseyed back over to the cart.

"How'd you like it?" I asked them.

"It was delectable!" said the tall fella.

"It was also quite delicious," said the short fella. "The best frozen custard I've ever tasted!"

"Gee, that's swell!" I said. "Will you say that on the radio?"

"Funny you should ask," said the tall fella. He pointed toward one of the posters that were tacked up around the park. "The Fourth of July is coming up in a few days. Lots of special events planned here at the zoo. Bob and I were thinking: Why not broadcast the whole shindig, live on the radio? And why not right here, next to Sparky's custard cart and Monkey Island?"

"That's right," said Bob. "What could be more patriotic than monkeys and frozen custard?"

"If you're gonna talk about Sparky's *custard* on the radio, you'd better tell your *listeners* what's in it," said a loud voice behind me.

I knew that voice. I did not like that voice.

The short fella reached out to shake hands. "You must be Sparky!"

Happy laughed his evil laugh. "Happy Harold's my name. And if you wanna know what good custard *really* tastes like, you'd better come on over to *my* cart. Because you'd be quite *surprised* to find out what Sparky's secret ingredient really is."

That got people's attention. A murmur went around the zoo like rolling thunder.

Happy kept going. "In fact, I think you'd better announce it on the *radio*, because I think the *parents* of this good city will want to know that their kids are eating custard made with *whiskey*."

I could've sworn that the entire zoo fell silent. For a few seconds, even the monkeys stopped chattering.

Finally the short radio fella said, "You don't say?"

The tall fella said, "No wonder it was so delicious."

I couldn't let this happen. "It's not whiskey!" I hollered.

"Oh, no?" said Happy. "What is it, then?"

"I'm not telling!" I said. "It's a secret!"

"*Aha!*" hollered Happy, as if that proved his point.

Ma nudged me aside. "Excuse me, Mr. Happy Harold. You want to know the secret ingredient? Maybe, if you ask me nice, I will tell you."

Happy looked at her sideways. "All right," he said, taking the bait. "What's the secret ingredient, *please*? And don't say 'marshmallows.'"

"*Hmph!*" said Ma. "I'm not telling you!" And she stomped away.

"I knew it!" said Happy, and he stomped away in the other direction.

There we stood with our hands in our pockets. Me and those two radio fellas.

"No whiskey, huh?" asked Bob finally.

I shook my head. "Nope."

"Ah, well." He rocked on his feet, and then he said, "Maybe Sparky oughta try whipping up a batch?"

"I don't think so," I told him.

"Ah, well."

"Say, kid," said Ray, leaning closer and lowering his voice. He twitched a thumb toward the pavilion. "Do you know why that custard lady is wearing a disguise?"

There was Ma, pacing and muttering to herself. It wasn't hard to spot her, with her dark glasses, that big ol' map-of-Greece scarf on her head, and her blue apron with SPARKY'S splashed across the bib in big white letters.

I love my mother with all my heart. I wouldn't trade her for anyone else in the whole wide world.

But that doesn't mean I know how to explain her.

So I said, "Something about monkeys escaping in 1929," and I turned to serve the next person in line.

The radio fellas gave each other a puzzled look. "If you say so," said the tall fella. "Come on, Bob. Let's go talk to Charley Stankey about our idea."

"Thanks a lot for the custard, kid," said the short fella. "See ya on the Fourth of July!" And the two of them ambled off to find Mr. Stankey.

That's when everything finally sank in. Holy smokes! The Fourth of July is already the best day of the whole summer. Parades. Flags. Concerts. Fireworks. And now Sparky's Frozen Custard, and the zoo, featured on the radio! The best day of the summer was about to get even better.

Someone tapped me on the shoulder. It was Ma, back to her old self. "What happens while I was gone?" she asked, watching as the radio fellas walked away.

"It's all set," I told her. "We're gonna be on the radio! Is it okay if I run to Sparky's and tell Uncle Spiro?"

"*Neh, neh,* and bring more custard," she said, and then she tugged at my sleeve. "But, Nicky, why those radio men were pointing at me?"

What could I say? "Um . . . they told me they like your scarf."

She stood up tall and lifted her chin. "Next time I will show them where I was born. It's here somewhere," she said, pointing in the vicinity of her left ear. And then she went back to serving custard and pinching cheeks.

CHAPTER

30

FROSTY FREEZE CUSTARD WAS A BONA-FIDE HIT, all right. But Frosty himself was an even bigger hit. Ever since his escape, that polar bear had more visitors than any other animal at the zoo. Which was kind of silly, because he was still the same old Frosty.

But then again, he wasn't.

He used to be Frosty, the cuddly white bear who loved marshmallows.

Now he was Frosty, the enormous black bear with white fur who might show up on your doorstep and decide that *you* taste better than marshmallows.

Like I said: still the same old Frosty.

On top of all that, exactly *how* he'd gotten out was still a mystery, which I suppose made folks a little nervous.

But mostly, it made them curious. All day, every day, people crammed around his fence, waving at him and taking his picture. Uncle Spiro called it "Frosty frenzy."

Now, on the way to tell Uncle Spiro the news about the Fourth of July, I took a quick detour to check on Frosty. Someone in the crowd tossed him a marshmallow, and he sat up on his hind legs and caught it in his mouth. Which was very entertaining, but also a little embarrassing for Frosty, if you ask me.

Anyway, I guess it was only a matter of time before some smart aleck decided to find out if Frosty the polar bear liked Frosty Freeze custard.

Something in the back of my mind told me it wouldn't be a good idea. There was the rule against feeding the animals, of course. But also, I remembered what the radio fellas had said:

Frosty had cavities.

I don't know about you, but I had a cavity once. It didn't really bother me at first. To be honest, I hardly noticed it—until I bit down on an ice cube. That sent a bolt of jagged lightning from my tooth to the top of my head and down to my toes.

Ma took me to see the dentist the next day. For once, I was happy to go.

And so now, when some grubby kid hurled a cup of

Frosty Freeze custard across the moat and into Frosty's enclosure, all I could think was, Uh-oh.

Frosty sniffed the custard. He tried a small lick.

"Isn't he cute?" squealed one little girl.

Frosty sniffed again. He took a bigger lick.

"Go ahead, Frosty, eat it all up!" hollered another kid.

The crowd held its breath.

And then, it happened. Frosty chomped on that custard, paper cup and all. He sat back and chewed.

The crowd cheered and laughed.

Then Frosty—the black bear with white fur—reared up, spit out the cup of custard, and *roared*.

"He's gone mad!" screamed one lady. Poor ol' Frosty tore around his enclosure, swinging his huge head from side to side and howling in pain.

"He's gonna bust out again!" hollered someone else.

He didn't bust out, of course. He couldn't. Like Mr. Stankey had said, the dry moat around Frosty's enclosure was too deep. Too wide. Too steep. After that first jolt of pain, poor ol' Frosty stumbled to a shady corner at the back of his enclosure, lay down, and curled into a ball.

The crowd let out scattered sounds of disappointment, and then one by one they wandered away.

"I guess he doesn't like Frosty Freeze," said someone. "Go figure."

And after that, no one bothered tossing custard to

Frosty. I'd like to think it was because they didn't want to cause him more pain. But probably it was because no one wanted to waste a perfectly good cup of custard on a polar bear with a toothache.

LATER THAT DAY I WAS HELPING MA AS USUAL WHEN Ace showed up, breathing hard and cradling an armful of custard cups.

"What's with you?" I asked him.

He juggled his load. "I'm dumping all the strawberry custard. Want some?"

"Keep your voice down! We got paying customers here." I pulled him away from Sparky's cart. "Why are you dumping Happy's custard?"

"Not all of it," said Ace. "Only the strawberry. I'm following orders!"

"Happy told you to throw away his custard?"

"He told us—*ahem*—'I want all this strawberry custard

gone by the end of the day!' And then he left."

I pointed at the sign above Happy's cart that said STRAWBERRY CUSTARD! GOING FAST! "Don't you think he meant you're supposed to *sell* it?"

"Oh, for sure," agreed Ace. "But Pete said to dump it. And when Happy's not around, Pete's in charge."

"Isn't Happy gonna blow his top when he finds out?"

Ace shrugged. "At least he'll have a reason for a change."

I couldn't argue with that. But I had to wonder what Pete was up to.

"Hey, punk!" called Pete from over at Happy's cart. "Hurry it up, before Happy gets back!"

I waited for the fists to fly, which is what happens whenever Pete calls Ace a punk. But instead, Ace just gave Pete a thumbs-up. "I gotta keep moving," he told me.

"I can't believe you're letting Pete get away with that."

"I can always punch him later," said Ace. "But right now, we both hate Happy more than we hate each other. He's been hollering at us all day, and me and Pete have had enough." He scurried over to the trash barrel next to Monkey Island and tossed in his entire armload of strawberry custard.

But then he stopped. He leaned over the fence and looked down into the Monkey Island moat. He motioned me over.

"Look!" said Ace. "It's Penny's little monkey pal."

Sure enough, there was Maxene, swimming in the moat, wiggling her fuzzy eyebrows at us.

"Has she been watching you?" I asked him. (That's one of the weird things about being at the zoo, by the way. There you are, watching all these animals, and they're on the other side of the fence, watching you. It makes you wonder: Who's really on display, anyway?)

"Oh, she's been watching me, all right," said Ace. "You know strawberry custard is her favorite."

"How would I know that?" I asked him. "How do *you* know that?"

But he just said, "Watch this."

He reached back into the trash barrel and pulled out one of the cups of strawberry custard. He made sure no one was looking, and then he chucked the cup into the moat.

Maxene grabbed it with one hand, like she was Joe DiMaggio in the outfield. She swam with it to the island and grabbed a long stick just in time to defend herself from another monkey, who apparently also wanted strawberry custard.

Maxene finally managed to chase off the other monkey. She stashed the stick behind a rock, pulled the cardboard lid off the cup like an old pro, and settled down to slurp her custard in peace.

But then I wondered about something. "Do you suppose a monkey could use a stick like that to haul itself out of the moat and over the fence?"

Ace thought for a minute. "If they could do that, don't you think they would've done it by now?"

He had a good point. But it made me think about the monkey escaping in 1929. Pop had said that no one ever did figure out how it had gotten out.

"Nicky!" called Ma from across the way.

"I gotta go," I said.

"Hey, punk!" called Pete.

"Me too," said Ace.

And we both got back to work.

CHAPTER

32

ACE SPENT THE REST OF THE AFTERNOON DEPOS-iting cups of strawberry custard into various trash barrels around the zoo. And every time he passed Monkey Island, he tossed another cup to Maxene.

"You're gonna get caught," I told him. "The zookeepers are making the rounds."

But did he listen? No, he did not.

Did he get caught? Yes, he did. By the head zookeeper himself.

"Do you see that sign, young man?" said Mr. Stankey, cornering Ace between the trash barrel and the fence. "It says 'Don't Feed the Animals.' Do you know *why* you shouldn't feed the animals?"

Ace opened his mouth to take a guess, but apparently Mr. Stankey wasn't expecting an answer, because he kept talking. "For one thing, they'll lose their natural fear of humans. Eventually, they'll do whatever it takes to get their paws on that food."

Behind him, Maxene was doing the backstroke in the moat, making eyes at Ace.

I probably should've tried coming to Ace's rescue. But I decided that, all things considered, it was best to blend into the scenery. Besides, I really wanted to find out what would happen next.

Mr. Stankey kept going. "We work hard to provide a balanced and nutritious diet for the animals in this zoo. Are you an expert in monkey nutrition, young man? Well, I can assure you, good monkey nutrition does not include ice cream."

"Custard," said Ace.

"What?"

"It's not ice cream," explained Ace. "It's frozen custard."

Mr. Stankey narrowed his eyes at Ace. "Nevertheless," he said in that voice grown-ups use when they want to sound like they're being patient, when really they're not. Then, out of the corner of his eye, he finally noticed Maxene. She was still watching Ace, and then (I could've sworn) she waved at him.

Mr. Stankey blinked twice at Maxene, and then he

continued his lecture. "Take a look at that little monkey. If every child who comes along feeds ice cr—frozen custard to that little monkey, what do you suppose will happen?"

"Fat monkey?" guessed Ace.

"That's the least of it!" said Mr. Stankey. "That little monkey will develop a sweet tooth. She'll decide that she doesn't want her carefully selected, nutritious diet, because she'll have developed a preference for chocolate custard!"

"Strawberry," squeaked Ace.

"What?"

"She hates chocolate. She doesn't mind vanilla, or even Frosty Freeze. But strawberry is definitely her favorite."

I waited for Mr. Stankey to ask Ace how he knew all that, but by now the wind had gone out of his sails. He heaved a long, exasperated sigh. "Please, young man. I'm begging you. My job is hard enough without having to chase you kids and scold you all the time. And it's not only kids! You have no idea how many adults I scold on a daily basis. 'Don't throw peanuts to the elephant!' 'Don't throw marshmallows to the polar bear!' Do you realize how lucky we are to have a polar bear at this zoo? A huge, fierce beast, with teeth like daggers and paws the size of dinner plates. In its natural habitat, it will eat an entire seal. Raw! And people are feeding it *marshmallows*? I ask you—what is wrong with people?"

Ace gulped and said helpfully, "But Frosty sure is cute when he sits up and begs for marshmallows."

"Cute? *Cute?* Now Frosty has cavities! A polar bear shouldn't have cavities! Do you think seals contain an over-abundance of sugar? Not to mention: Do you know how hard it is to find a dentist who will fill a polar bear's teeth? And how much he charges? It's highway robbery, that's what it is!" Mr. Stankey took a breath. His face had gone an interesting shade of purple.

"Gee, Mr. Stankey," said Ace. "That's too bad. Poor ol' Frosty."

"Poor ol' Frosty is right!" said Mr. Stankey. "And the dentist can only come on the weekend, and he'll need at least two zookeepers to assist with sedation, which means I'll have to pay them overtime. *You* try running a zoo some-time!" And he stomped away, muttering something about frozen custard and marshmallows.

"Jeepers," I said to Ace. "Are you okay?"

"I'm fine." He tucked in his shirt and straightened his bow tie. "But I sure do hope there's a *Mrs.* Stankey, because somebody really needs to keep an eye on him."

CHAPTER

33

THE NEXT DAY AFTER BREAKFAST, ME AND ACE wandered over to see what Penny was up to. And to see if there might be donuts.

We found her sitting on the top step of her front porch, with her elbows on her knees and her head in her hands.

"Hiya, Penny," we called.

When she saw us coming, she sat up straight and swiped at her eyes. They were all red and shiny.

"Are you crying?" said Ace, plopping down next to her.

She sniffed, and shrugged, and nodded.

I never know what to do when a girl cries. I don't have any sisters to practice on, and Ma never cries—she's the kind of person who makes *other* people cry.

So I sat on the step and felt my hands getting sweaty, like they always do when I'm nervous.

Ace, on the other hand, has loads of experience. His little sister is always crying about something.

"What's the matter?" he said, resting a hand on Penny's shoulder. "No donuts today? That makes me wanna cry too."

Penny gave another big sniff. "It's not because of donuts."

"Did something happen on your paper route?" I asked.

"Was it a dog?" said Ace. "I tell ya, some of those mongrels are ferocious. I'd rather bump into a polar bear."

Penny shook her head again and blew her nose into a little pink hanky. She sounded like someone stepping on a mouse. "The route was okay," she said finally. "But at the shack . . ."

She made the squeaky-mouse noise into the hanky again.

I couldn't stand it. "What happened at the shack?"

She took a deep breath. "I'm gonna be fired, that's what."

Holy smokes.

"Fired? Why?"

"Why do you think?" said Penny. "Because I'm a girl."

Poor ol' Penny. She'd been through this before. One time, she was kicked out of a batboy contest because she's not actually a boy. In other words, even though it wasn't written down anywhere, the rule was loud and clear: No Girls Allowed.

Rules. I'll admit that some of them make sense, like "Go to school" or "Do not feed the animals." But it seems like other rules are invented just to remind kids that we're not in charge. "No custard before dinner" or "Take a bath once a week whether you need it or not." And some rules, I swear, are invented to remind some people that they'll never be in charge. Ever since I met Penny, I've learned that "No girls allowed" is one of those rules. Girls aren't supposed to be anything that has "boy" in the name, like batboy or altar boy or paperboy—even if they're good at it. It doesn't make any sense. And it's not fair. There shouldn't be rules that make people wish they were someone else.

"How do you know you're gonna be fired?" I asked her.

Penny tugged at a braid and wiped her eyes. "It's the end of the month, right? Well, it turns out there's a prize for the paperboy who makes all his collections during the month."

"Who told you that?" said Ace.

Penny sniffed. "The supervisor made an announcement this morning, when everyone was picking up their papers for the day. It turns out that this month's winner . . . was me."

"That's swell!" I said. "What's the prize?"

She shrugged. "He didn't say. He just said the winner could pick it up at the end of the shift today."

"Did you?" I asked her, but she shook her head.

"Why not?" said Ace.

"I never did tell him that you turned your route over to me," said Penny. "He still thinks *you're* delivering papers and making the collections. He wants to give the prize to *you*. When I show up to claim the prize, he'll fire me for sure."

Ace scratched his head. "You mean he hasn't noticed a girl picking up a stack of papers every day? And turning in the route money at the end of the week?"

Penny shrugged again. "I don't dress like a girl when I deliver papers," she said. "I wear my old overalls, and I stuff my hair under a baseball cap so I don't have to bother brushing it early in the morning."

She had a point. When they're wearing overalls, every twelve-year-old kid looks like every other twelve-year-old kid from the neck down. It's Penny's mop of hair that gives her away. And if her hair was covered up, I could see how the newspaper supervisor wouldn't give her a second glance.

I had an idea.

"Why can't he keep thinking it's Ace's route?" I said. "He'll give the prize to Ace, and Ace will give it to you. And you won't get fired."

But Penny shook her head. "It'd be . . . lying. Somehow it would be worse than just avoiding him. Plus, it stinks to work hard and earn a prize, and then let someone else take the credit."

"It's either that or get fired," I told her. "Listen, take Ace with you right now to get your prize. He'll back up your story."

"I don't know . . . ," she said.

"Why not?" Ace said. "Don't you trust me?"

"I trust you," said Penny. "It's your mouth I'm worried about."

"Gee, thanks," he muttered.

"We'll both go with you," I told her. "And if Ace starts to blab something dumb, I'll step on his foot to stop him."

Penny thought about that. "Okay," she said finally. She didn't sound too happy about it, but at least she wasn't crying anymore.

To be honest, I wasn't happy about it either. But what else could we do?

So me and Ace each grabbed an elbow, and we marched her up the sidewalk to claim her prize.

CHAPTER

34

ACE BUSTED INTO THE NEWSPAPER SHACK LIKE he owned the place. "Hiya, boss! I'm here to pick up my prize." He turned back to give me and Penny a huge wink.

The supervisor looked up from counting stacks of newspapers. He pulled a toothpick out of his mouth and pointed it at Ace. "Ain't you the kid who delivered his first collection in a custard container? Late?"

"That's me," said Ace.

"*You're* this month's winner?"

"Yes sir," said Ace. Penny and I nodded helpfully.

The supervisor clenched the toothpick in his teeth and squinted up at the announcement posted on his bulletin board. "You're . . . Horace Nowicky?"

"Yeah," admitted Ace.

The supervisor shuffled through some papers on an upturned milk crate that he used as a desk. "Here they are," he said, handing an envelope over to Ace. "Two tickets to the ball game a week from Saturday. Right behind the Mudpuppies' dugout. A three-dollar value!"

"Jeepers!" said Ace. "For me?"

I coughed. Ace sighed and handed the envelope over to Penny.

The supervisor didn't seem to notice. "I'm real impressed, Horace. You're the only paperboy who collected from all his accounts—even the ones past due. And you've only been on the job for a couple of weeks!"

Ace opened his mouth. I stepped on his foot. He shut his mouth again.

The supervisor kept talking. "Yes sir, I'm real impressed. I even got notes in some of the payment envelopes. Usually I only get notes when someone messes up." He shuffled through his papers again and picked up some scraps that he'd paper-clipped together. "Listen to this: 'My newspapers have been on time every day for the first time all summer.'"

Ace grinned and said, "The early bird gets the worm, sir." He turned and gave me and Penny another big fat wink.

"Here's another one," said the supervisor, flipping the page. "'My newspaper gets tucked inside the screen door on rainy days.'"

Ace puffed out his chest. "Nothing worse than a wet newspaper, sir."

Penny sighed loudly.

The supervisor kept going. "Here's my favorite: 'My dog really loves the new paperboy.'"

"That does it!" said Penny.

"What's wrong, honey?" said the supervisor. "Aren't you happy for Horace?"

"No!" said Penny. "I mean, yes! I mean—"

Ace nudged me. "And she was worried about *my* mouth."

I stepped on his foot again, just because. It might cost her everything she'd worked for, but I could tell that this was something Penny needed to do.

Her voice was shaky but strong. "The thing is, Ace didn't deliver those papers, or make those collections." She lifted her chin. "I did."

The supervisor's eyebrows went up. "*You* did?"

Penny gulped. "It's my paper route."

He chewed his toothpick and shook a thumb at Ace. "This raggedy kid says it's his route."

"It was," said Penny. "But he turned the route over to me last week."

"So all these nice notes are about you?"

Penny blushed. "I guess so."

The man narrowed his eyes at Ace. "Let me get this

straight. You turned over your entire paper route to this young lady here, and you didn't tell me?"

Ace's ears turned red.

Penny looked the supervisor straight in the eye. "He didn't tell you because we both know you wouldn't let a girl have a paper route."

The supervisor blinked. His toothpick shifted from one side of his mouth to the other. And then he said, "Do your parents know what you're doing?"

Penny nodded.

"And it's okay with them?"

She nodded again.

"Well, I'll be a monkey's uncle." And then he shrugged. "I suppose if it's okay with your folks, then why not? I'm not about to fire my best paperboy for being a paper*girl*." He slapped Penny on the back. "Keep up the good work, son, and enjoy that ball game!"

CHAPTER

35

A LITTLE WHILE LATER, ACE CLIPPED ON HIS BOW tie and trudged off to Happy's cart. It was time for me to go to Uncle Spiro's shop to load up the Radio Flyer with custard and wheel it to the zoo. Penny offered to come with me. (Except this time we didn't need a police escort. Which was a little disappointing, to be honest.)

We'd been so busy helping Penny not get fired from her paper route that I'd forgotten to tell her all the crazy stuff that had happened yesterday after she went home to see her big sister with the broken pinky finger.

"There's gonna be a live radio broadcast from the zoo on the Fourth of July," I said. "They're gonna set up right next to Sparky's cart!"

"I know!" said Penny. "Uncle Spiro told us."

"He did? Who the heck is 'us'?"

"Me and Josie," said Penny. "She wanted to celebrate coming home by getting custard, so we went to Sparky's."

"Yesterday? But your ma made donuts."

"We went for custard after the donuts."

You had to admire girls who could pack away donuts and custard on the same day. "Josie really likes custard, huh?"

"I think she really likes your uncle," said Penny, and then she blushed. And then I blushed too. For some stupid reason.

When we got to the zoo, we noticed new signs posted everywhere. They said:

POSITIVELY NO FEEDING THE ANIMALS!
VIOLATORS WILL BE FINED
$10 FOR EACH INFRACTION.
—BY ORDER OF C. W. STANKEY, HEAD ZOOKEEPER

"Holy smokes," I said. "Ace really got under Mr. Stankey's skin."

"That's all because of Ace?" said Penny, who looked surprised, until she remembered we were talking about Ace.

I filled her in on how Ace had gotten collared by Mr. Stankey himself for tossing strawberry custard to Maxene the monkey.

"Golly," said Penny. "I thought it was because of all the trash." She nodded toward Monkey Island.

Now it was my turn to look surprised, but she was right. There was garbage all over Monkey Island—even more than usual.

I hate to say this, but there's trash on Monkey Island on most days. The zoo is in the middle of the city park, which means that anyone can come and go at any hour of the day or night. And apparently, they do. Because on most days at opening time, there's a scattering of trash on Monkey Island from the night before. It doesn't happen only at night, either. I've seen people tossing all kinds of things to the monkeys in broad daylight: Cracker Jack. Peanuts. Even stuff like balls and pencils and little mirrors, to see what the monkeys will do with them. No wonder poor ol' Mr. Stankey is always so cranky.

And today, in addition to all the usual junk that gets thrown onto Monkey Island, there was a whole lot of one particular item.

Custard cups.

Uh-oh.

Two zookeepers were out there in coveralls, rubber gloves, and waders, trying to clean it up, while the monkeys kept trying to grab it back. They were drawing a pretty good crowd.

I leaned over toward Penny. "How many custard cups do you suppose are out there?" I squeaked.

She pointed a finger, counting. Finally she said, "A couple of dozen, at least."

Uh-oh.

"That's weird."

"Why?" said Penny as we parked the wagon next to the custard cart. "You just said that Ace tossed custard to the monkeys. Hi, Mrs. Spirakis!"

"Hello, *koukla mou*," said Ma, who was waiting for us as usual.

We hoisted the cooler chest onto the cart. "Ace only tossed three or four cups to Maxene," I whispered to Penny. "Not dozens. He threw most of them into the trash barrels." Then I explained to her about Ace and Pete dumping all of Happy's strawberry custard.

"Why did they do that?"

"To get even with Happy for hollering all the time." I shook my head. "Somebody else must've dug those cups out of the trash barrels overnight and tossed them onto Monkey Island."

"Who?"

"Good question."

Just then, here came Mr. Stankey, in his Parks Department uniform, ranger hat, and steel-toed boots. He marched up to Sparky's custard cart and said to Ma, "I need to speak to Sparky—I mean, Spiro—right away."

Ma looked at him over the top of her sunglasses. "Who are you?"

Mr. Stankey stood up as tall as he could, which was only a little taller than Ma. "I'm in charge of this zoo."

She pointed across the path. "You are in charge of those monkeys?"

Mr. Stankey blinked at her. "That's right."

She narrowed her eyes at him. "Were you here in 1929?"

"No! Why?"

"In 1929, the man in charge did not keep an eye on those monkeys," said Ma, tying her giant scarf tighter under her chin. "I hope you are keeping an eye."

Mr. Stankey rubbed the back of his neck. "Please, ma'am. Where's Spiro?"

I stepped up and said, "He's at the shop. I can go get him if you want."

Now Mr. Stankey gave me the once-over. I wondered if he recognized me from yesterday, when I was trying not to get noticed while he was hollering at Ace. But he just said, "You do that, young man. I need to see him right away."

Uh-oh.

"Sure thing. What's this about, if you don't mind my asking?"

Mr. Stankey gave a sigh. "I'm afraid I have to shut down this custard cart."

CHAPTER

36

"YOU CAN'T SHUT US DOWN!" SAID UNCLE SPIRO. His face was already red from running all the way from the shop, but somehow it was getting even redder.

"I have no choice," said Mr. Stankey. "I'm responsible for the well-being of the animals in this zoo. Do you know how many custard cups were found on Monkey Island this morning? Twenty-seven, that's how many. This sort of thing simply cannot be tolerated."

"But it's not my fault!" protested Uncle Spiro. "I can't help what people do with my custard after they buy it."

He was right. And it wasn't even his custard. I knew whose custard it was.

"What about *their* custard cups?" I said, pointing toward Happy's cart.

From across the way, Ace waved. "Hiya, Mr. Stankey! Remember me?"

Mr. Stankey's eyes narrowed. But he just shook his head and said, "That cart is not my concern."

I couldn't believe my ears. "Why not?"

Mr. Stankey pointed. "That cart is not officially on zoo property, and therefore—I'm sorry to say—I have no authority over it. I do have authority over this cart. Excessive numbers of custard cups have been deposited on Monkey Island, and it has to stop."

Ma tugged Uncle Spiro's sleeve. "Listen to this little man, Spiro. He is in charge of those monkeys. Remember what happened in 1929."

I had an idea. "In that case, we'll wheel our cart off zoo property. And then you won't have authority over us, either."

Mr. Stankey spluttered. "This cart *is* zoo property, young man. I will not allow it to be removed from the premises."

Penny nudged me. "He's right, Nick. Remember how it was stored in the shed behind his office?"

"Then we'll build our own cart," I said. "How hard could that be?"

Uncle Spiro put a hand on my shoulder. "It's not just the cart, Nick. If I go off zoo property, I'd need a vendor's license from the city. That takes weeks. The Fourth of July is in a few days."

This was not going well. We were running out of ideas.

"What about your ten-dollar fine, Mr. Stankey?" tried Penny. "That should keep people from throwing anything onto Monkey Island, even custard cups."

Mr. Stankey groaned. "I don't have the staff to enforce those signs, especially after hours. No, I need to cover all my bases here. Ever since that unfortunate polar bear incident—"

"You mean when Frosty escaped?" I said.

Mr. Stankey coughed. "Yes. Ever since then, reporters won't stop calling me. Second-guessing my decisions. Questioning our safety measures. If they get wind of the mess on Monkey Island, I'll never hear the end of it. I could lose my job!" He turned to the people waiting in line. "This custard cart is closed!"

You should've seen their faces. But those sad faces were nothing compared with Uncle Spiro's.

"What about the Fourth of July?" he said. "The radio broadcast? I've been making extra custard! It's my biggest day of the year! You can't do this!"

"I'm afraid I can," said Mr. Stankey. "I'm sorry." He turned to leave.

I couldn't let this happen. Uncle Spiro had worked too hard to lose his custard cart now.

"Wait a minute, Mr. Stankey!"

Mr. Stankey turned back around. He sighed heavily. "Yes, young man?"

I gulped. It was a crazy idea, and I didn't even know I'd been thinking it. But I had to try something.

"What if we can guarantee that no more custard cups end up on Monkey Island?"

Mr. Stankey frowned. "How are you going to do that?"

"Yeah, Nick," said Uncle Spiro. "How are we gonna do that?"

I kept going. "What if we give people a penny for every empty custard cup they bring back to the cart? Like you get for returning empty soda bottles."

"A deposit?" said Uncle Spiro. "Interesting. Except we don't charge a deposit."

"But we could," I said, thinking fast. "Sparky's custard is ten cents a cup, right? So, what if it's nine cents a cup, plus a one-cent deposit?" I gulped again. This would cost us. But it was better than getting shut down.

Uncle Spiro must have thought so too, because a smile bloomed on his face. "You know what, Nick? I think that could work—at least until we think of something better." He turned toward Mr. Stankey. "What do you say, Charley?"

Mr. Stankey scratched his chin, thinking. He looked over at Monkey Island. He looked at the line of disappointed people still waiting for frozen custard. He sighed.

"I suppose it's worth a try." Then he shook a finger at us. "But if there's even one custard cup on Monkey Island, the whole deal is off. And that includes cups from that cart." He pointed over toward Happy's.

"Don't worry," I said, sounding a lot more sure than I felt. "They'll pay a deposit too. They just don't know it yet."

CHAPTER
37

I T DIDN'T TAKE LONG FOR WORD TO GET OUT THAT Sparky's cart was paying a penny apiece for empty custard cups. We even paid for Happy's cups. That cost us extra, but we couldn't take any chances. One stray cup on Monkey Island, and we were done.

It's amazing what people will do for a penny. Pretty soon the line at Sparky's was almost as long as on the day we first served Frosty Freeze. Packs of kids even started roaming the zoo, trying to collect enough cups to get a free custard.

The place had never looked so neat.

And then something else happened. After spending all that time waiting in line for their penny, lots of folks figured, "What the heck? While I'm here, might as well buy some more custard." So even though we paid a penny a cup, we actually ended up selling even more custard than before.

It was swell.

Uncle Spiro needed to get back to the shop, but the rest of us had things under control. Ma served custard as usual, Penny offered to help collect the deposit money, and I bagged the empties to throw away at the end of the day.

After a while, Ace came running over, holding his pants up with one hand.

"Forgot your belt?" I said.

"The dog ate it."

"You don't have a dog."

"I didn't say it was *my* dog. Anyway, Happy wants to know if you're really paying a penny a cup for empties."

Penny crossed her arms. "Happy sent you over here to spy on us?"

Ace hitched up his pants. "It's not spying if you know I'm doing it."

That's when Ma hollered, "Bring your empty cup to Sparky's and get a penny! Only custard cups! No popcorn or soda cups! We are not made of pennies!"

Ace's eyes got wide. "It's true! What're you doing that for?"

I opened my mouth to explain everything, but then someone stepped on my foot, hard.

Penny. She gave me a glare and a tiny shake of her head.

And then I figured out what she was trying to say:

Don't tell Ace.

She was right. If we told Ace, Ace would tell Happy. And if Happy knew that (a) we were paying people for their empty custard cups because (b) even one lousy cup on Monkey Island would get us shut down, he'd probably (c) march right over and personally chuck a cup over the fence. And that would (d) be the end of Sparky's custard cart, once and for all.

I didn't want to keep Ace in the dark, but we couldn't risk telling him. Because everyone knows that Ace can't keep a secret.

"Um," I said, thinking fast. "Well. You know how the soda company pays a penny if you return their empty bottles? It's like that."

Ace frowned and adjusted his pants. "The soda company reuses the bottles. You can't do that with paper custard cups, can you?"

We all looked down at the sack full of empties. It had been discovered by a swarm of ants.

"Yuck," said Penny.

Ace took a closer look. "You're paying for Happy's cups too?"

"Um," I said again. Then I blurted the first thing that popped into my head. "Like Uncle Spiro says: Gotta stay a step ahead of the competition."

Ace bought it. He went back and told Happy, who did not like it one bit, especially when he saw *his* customers in *our* line with his empty cups. And more than a few of those customers were now buying *our* custard.

I guess Happy decided there was only one thing he could do. He started offering a penny for every empty cup too. Just like I'd predicted he would.

And in case you're wondering, I didn't have to worry about Ace spilling the beans after all. Because a few days later, I managed to do that all by myself.

CHAPTER

38

IT WAS FIVE O'CLOCK ON SATURDAY AFTERNOON. After we closed up shop, Ma headed home. I wheeled the custard cart into the storage shed for the night, and then I wandered over to Happy's cart to see what Ace was up to.

"Well, well, *well*," sneered Happy when he saw me coming. "Calling it quits already? I'm just gettin' *started*." He nodded to his long line of customers.

"All the zoo vendors close up at five o'clock," I told him. "It's Mr. Stankey's rule."

Happy snorted. "Out here on the *sidewalk*, I make my own rules. Of course, it's only *fair* that I get all the customers on a Saturday night. Your uncle's been stealing my customers ever since he opened his shop. *And* he stole my zoo concession."

"No one stole anything from you, Happy," I muttered.

"Oh no? When South Side Lenny's machine pulled up lame a couple of weeks ago, the zoo job should've been mine. But instead, Old Man Stankey gives the job to your rookie uncle." Happy's lip curled. "I don't forget stuff like that, kid."

"Uncle Spiro did not steal your zoo concession!" said Ace. Good old Ace.

"You stay out of this," Happy snarled at Ace. "Or I'll fire you. See what your ma has to say about that."

Ace gulped. Pete kept serving customers, pretending like he wasn't listening. So much for Pete being fed up with Happy.

Happy turned back to me. "Sparky stole my idea for a third flavor, too. He only invented *his* special flavor after I invented strawberry. And now I have to pay a penny for every sticky, disgusting, empty custard cup, and *that's* his fault too!"

Happy was twice my size, and more than twice my age. My folks had taught me to be respectful to grown-ups. But they had also taught me to stand up to bullies. So what are you supposed to do when the bully is a grown-up?

"Happy," I said, "you're full of beans."

He snorted again. "Oh yeah? Well, I happen to know

that Frosty Freeze is full of whiskey. Wait till I tell Old Man Stankey. He'll shut you down for good!"

Now I was mad.

"So what?" I snapped back. "Mr. Stankey already threatened to shut us down!"

Happy's eyebrows shot up. "What?"

"That's right," I said. "Mr. Stankey is already gonna shut us down if he finds any more custard cups on Monkey Island!"

Oops. Maybe I shouldn't have said that.

Ace gasped. Pete gave a low whistle.

And Happy's face spread into an evil grin. "Is that so?"

All of a sudden, I knew how Ace must have felt right before he barfed all over Happy's shoes.

I gulped down the sick feeling and said, "Don't you dare, Happy."

Happy waved a hand. "Don't worry, kid. I'm not gonna *do* anything." And then that evil grin of his got even bigger. "Not yet."

This was not going well.

"I gotta go," I told Ace, who was still standing there, speechless.

"That's right," Happy hollered after me as I hurried away. "Go tell that uncle of yours that I'm gonna strike when he least expects it!"

CHAPTER
39

I HURRIED THE TWO BLOCKS TO SPARKY'S CUSTARD Shop, even though I could think of a million things I'd rather do than tell Uncle Spiro what had just happened. Go to summer school. Spend the night in Frosty's enclosure. Help Ma with the ironing.

But Uncle Spiro had to know, *now*. I walked into the shop and blurted it out before I could change my mind.

Spiro dropped his scooper onto the floor with a clatter.

"What do you mean, *you told Happy*?" He hustled me to the back storage room, where he could holler at me in private. "You blabbed to Happy that one custard cup on Monkey Island puts us out of business?"

I nodded, but I couldn't look him in the eye. "Happy threatened to shut us down," I said. "He said he'd tell Mr. Stankey that Frosty Freeze is made with whiskey."

"That old story?" said Uncle Spiro in exasperation.

"That's when I told him that Mr. Stankey is already gonna shut us down . . . if he finds any more custard cups on Monkey Island. Ace and Pete heard it too."

"Why?" wailed Uncle Spiro. "Tomorrow is the Fourth of July! I've been working late every night this week, making extra custard. And now this happens?"

I tried to defend myself. "Happy was bad-mouthing Sparky's! He said that you've been stealing his customers. That he should've gotten the zoo concession instead of you. That you only invented Frosty Freeze after he invented strawberry. And now he's paying a deposit for empty custard cups, and he says that's your fault too. I couldn't just stand there and let him say that stuff!"

"You couldn't have waited one more day?" pleaded Uncle Spiro. "Everything's been going great all week! Not a single custard cup to be seen anywhere. How could you mess it up now?"

This wasn't fair. "What was I supposed to do? I was sticking up for *you*."

Uncle Spiro took a deep breath. Finally he said, "You're right, Nick. I'm sorry" He shook his head. "The nerve of that Happy, to pick on a kid." He started pacing the little room. "How long did it take Happy to toss a custard cup? About half a second, I'm guessing?"

"Happy didn't do anything," I said. "He just said . . . he'd strike when we least expect it."

"What the heck does that mean?" said Uncle Spiro.

I shrugged helplessly.

"Now what?" said Uncle Spiro. "Tomorrow is the biggest day of the year. And Happy's gonna do something to ruin it." He rubbed his forehead, thinking. "There's nothing I can do about it now. It's Saturday, so I'm stuck here at the shop until late. We'll just have to hope that Happy doesn't pull any tricks before tomorrow."

But I couldn't wait until tomorrow.

"I'm going back to the zoo," I said.

Uncle Spiro looked surprised. "What are you gonna do?"

"I don't know," I told him as I headed for the door. "But I'll think of something."

CHAPTER

40

So THERE I WAS, BACK OUT ON THE SIDEWALK. Behind me, inside Sparky's Custard Shop, I could hear the jukebox playing and the carefree voices of people whose summer was not falling apart.

That's when I saw Penny walking toward me up the sidewalk. "Hiya, Nick!" she called. "I'm going down to the newspaper shack to sort the Sunday supplements, so I don't have to do it in the morning. Wanna come with me? It won't take long."

"Nah. I need to get back to the zoo and keep tabs on Happy."

"Why? What happened?"

So I told her everything.

"I've never seen Uncle Spiro so upset," I said. "Not even when he got drafted into the army and had to go to war."

"Don't worry," said Penny, but her forehead was wrinkled. "I'll come find you as soon as I'm done," she promised, and she headed in the opposite direction.

So I walked the rest of the way to the zoo by myself, which gave me plenty of time to think about stuff. What did Happy mean by striking when we least expected it? All he had to do was chuck a cup of custard onto Monkey Island, and we'd be finished. But then I wondered: If that's what we *expected* him to do . . . would he do something else instead?

Tomorrow was the Fourth of July. I should've been thinking about eating too many hot dogs and finding the best spot to watch the fireworks with Ace and Penny. But instead, I kept thinking about how I'd messed everything up.

When I got to the zoo, red-white-and-blue bunting had been draped everywhere, ready for the big day tomorrow. The Monkey Island fence; the fence around Mountain Goat Mountain; even the rhinoceros yard was decorated with bunting. If I was in a better mood, I'd say that Tank the rhino looked very dignified. In fact, I'd say the whole place looked pretty spiffy.

But I wasn't in a better mood. I was in a terrible mood. Because it was only a matter of time before Happy would do something awful to seal our doom.

When I got to Happy's cart, Pete was there by himself, waiting on a little kid.

"A cup of strawberry?" squeaked the kid, holding out a dime.

Pete jerked a thumb toward a sign behind him:

COMING ON THE 4TH OF JULY!

BACK BY POPULAR DEMAND!

STRAWBERRY CUSTARD!

"Can't you read the sign, kid?"

"No. I'm five."

"Oh. No strawberry till tomorrow."

"Why not?"

"I dunno, kid! You want custard? We have vanilla and chocolate."

The little kid sighed. "Vanilla. I guess."

Pete gave the kid his custard. "Now beat it." Then he looked up and saw me. "What do you want?"

"Where's Ace?"

"That punk? Happy canned him."

"Canned?" I said. "What do you mean, 'canned'?"

"Fired," said Pete. "Sacked. Got the boot."

"I know what it means," I said. "Why? Because he tried to stick up for me?"

"Nope," said Pete. "For stealing."

Holy smokes.

But it didn't make any sense. "Ace wouldn't steal from anyone. Not even Happy."

Pete snorted. "It's not like he raided the cash box, knucklehead. Remember a few days ago? When all that strawberry custard went into the trash?"

And onto Monkey Island.

"Yeah?"

"Well," said Pete, "last night, Happy counted up his receipts for the week. The custard that went out didn't match up with the money that came in. He was three whole dollars short."

Holy cow. Now it made sense.

Except for one thing. "How come Ace is the one who got fired? He said throwing away all the strawberry custard was your idea!"

Pete grinned. "Happy doesn't know that. Besides, he can't fire both of us."

"So, you let Ace take the blame."

"Better him than me."

The nerve of that Pete. One of these days, he'd get what was coming to him.

But I had other things to worry about right now.

"Where'd Happy go?"

"Beats me," said Pete. "He didn't toss custard onto Monkey Island, if that's what you're wondering. Oh, he wanted to. But the place is crawling with zookeepers getting ready for tomorrow. Happy said something about biding his time."

"Biding his time?" I said. "What does that mean?" Because this time, I really didn't know what that meant.

"How should I know?" said Pete. "Get lost. I'm busy."

I had to find Ace. I turned toward the zoo entrance, grumbling to myself, when I tripped over something on the sidewalk. A stupid stick. Must've fallen out of the big tree that shaded Happy's cart. I was about to kick it off the sidewalk and onto the grass, but then I stopped and took a closer look.

All the bark had been stripped off it.

I looked into the branches of the tree high overhead. They were healthy and full of leaves.

A stripped stick. Exactly like the one used to prop Frosty's door open the day he escaped. And this one was on the ground right next to Happy's cart, under a perfectly healthy tree.

Just then, Penny came charging up the sidewalk. I was about to show her the stick when she said, "Well, that's it. I'm going to be fired after all!"

CHAPTER

41

I FORGOT ALL ABOUT THE STICK.

"Fired? Why?"

We walked over toward Monkey Island and sat down on a bench.

"Someone on my route complained about a girl taking a boy's job," said Penny. "The supervisor told me that if he keeps getting complaints, he'll have to fire me, whether he wants to or not."

"Holy smokes," I said. "What are you gonna do?"

She shrugged. "I need to think about it."

So I told Penny all about Ace getting canned/sacked/fired by Happy. Somehow, I thought it would make her feel better. But she said, "This summer is going to heck in a handbasket."

We both stared out at the monkeys for a while. Then Penny sat up straight and pointed along the path. "There he is."

Sure enough, here came Ace. His white shirt was rumpled, untucked, and custard stained. His soda-jerk hat was missing, and his clip-on bow tie was hanging loose from his collar.

"We've been looking for you," I told him. "Pete said that Happy fired you!"

"Can you believe it?" said Ace. "And Happy says I owe him three dollars for the missing strawberry custard!" He plopped down onto the bench.

"Pay him out of the money you've earned so far this summer," I said. "It'll be worth it, to get him off your back."

"What money? I'm broke."

"You haven't saved anything?" said Penny.

He gave her a look. "Money's not for saving. Money's for spending."

"What the heck did you spend it on?" I asked.

He thought about it. "Custard, mostly."

"Why?" I said. "You get all the free custard you want from Uncle Spiro."

He gave me an exasperated look. "Yeah, but Happy makes me pay."

"You get free custard from Sparky's *and* you buy it from Happy?"

"A fella's gotta eat!" Ace dropped his head into his hands. "Where am I gonna get three dollars?"

Since I was Ace's best friend, it was my job to make him feel better. To tell him that things weren't so bad. That everything would look better in the morning.

But who was I kidding?

I said, "You'll have to earn it, I guess."

"How?" he moaned. "I don't have a job, remember? My ma's gonna kill me."

"We'll think of something," said Penny, which was pretty nice of her, considering the bad news she'd just gotten.

But Ace didn't know about that. "Easy for you to say. You haven't had to put up with Happy Harold. You weren't double-crossed by that snake Pete. You have a nice, easy paper route."

Penny's eyes got wide and her face got red. "Easy? You quit that paper route after one week! I bailed you out! And this is the thanks I get?"

"Bailed me out?" said Ace. "I *gave* you that paper route! And now you get Mudpuppies tickets and everything! *You* oughta be thanking *me*!"

"Is that so?" said Penny. "Well, as it turns out, I'm going to be fired from that nice, easy paper route after all. Does that make you happy?"

I had to say something. The three of us were a team. We shouldn't be hollering at each other or blaming each other. We should be there for each other.

So, what did I say?

What I said was:

"Let me tell you how *my* summer is going. First, you both go off and get a paper route without me. And then Ace quits the paper route and goes to work for our worst enemy! And now, Sparky's Frozen Custard Cart will be shut down for good, and it's all my fault because after three whole days keeping Ace in the dark so he wouldn't blab to Happy, I opened my own big fat mouth!"

Ace gasped. "You're keeping secrets from me?"

Oops.

"What was I supposed to do?" I said in my own defense. "Everyone knows you can't keep your mouth shut!"

We all sat there, red in the face and breathing hard.

Finally I blurted out exactly what everyone was thinking.

"This summer stinks!"

CHAPTER

42

THERE I WAS EARLY ON SUNDAY MORNING, STILL in bed. Today was the Fourth of July, which should've been the best day of the whole summer. Concerts. Flags. Fireworks. But instead, Penny was hanging on to her paper route by a fingernail, Ace owed three dollars he didn't have, and I'd single-handedly told Happy Harold how to get Sparky's custard cart shut down for good.

How had things fallen apart so fast? Me and Ace and Penny were supposed to be a team. Doing stuff together. On the lookout for polar bears. Solving the mystery of Lenny's wrecked custard machine, and Frosty's unlocked door, and the stick with no bark. But instead, we'd ended up fuming at each other.

Music floated up the stairs from the kitchen radio. It was Pop's favorite program: *Ray and Bob's Sunday-Morning Serenade*. From the sound of it, this week's theme was patriotic music. To put people in the holiday mood.

But it made my mood worse. I pulled the covers over my head and tried to forget all the ways the summer had gone wrong.

Then, in the middle of a rousing rendition of "Yankee Doodle Dandy," the music scratched to a stop.

That was weird. I lowered the covers and sat up in bed.

We interrupt this program to bring you a special bulletin.

RAY: Shortly after five o'clock this morning, a full-grown polar bear was reported missing from the city zoo.

BOB: Are you reading an old report, Ray?

RAY: I'm afraid not, Bob. This is fresh off the wire. According to authorities, the half-ton critter—

BOB: Frosty! His name is Frosty.

RAY: —has been roaming the streets for the last hour and has now been located in a residential neighborhood. As we speak, officers are rushing to the scene, where the bear has cornered a local papergirl—

"Papergirl?"

I got dressed as quick as I could, raced downstairs, and busted into the kitchen. Uncle Spiro was already putting his shoes on.

"Did you hear?" I asked him.

"Yep. Let's go." He gulped the last of his coffee and headed for the back door.

RAY: All residents of the neighborhoods around the zoo are urged to stay indoors until further notice.

Ma blocked the kitchen door. "Did you hear that?"

"But, Ma," I told her, "they said 'papergirl.' That's Penny!"

Ma's eyes got wide. "That nice girl with all the hair? Eaten by a polar bear?"

"I don't know, Ma! But she needs help!"

"What kind of world we are living in?" muttered Ma.

Pop looked out from behind his newspaper. "Nicky? Does your little friend deliver *our* morning paper?"

"I think so. Why?"

Pop nodded approvingly. "I must remember to give her a bigger tip."

Uncle Spiro and I looked at Pop's newspaper and then at each other.

I ran for the front door.

"Nicky!" hollered Ma. "Don't go out there!"

But Frosty wasn't on our porch, and neither was Penny. And they weren't anywhere on our block.

I ran back to the kitchen. "They're not out there," I reported.

Uncle Spiro grabbed the car keys from their hook by the door. "Don't worry, Athena. We'll stay in the car. That Nash is built like a tank."

"Hurry back, Spiro," said Pop, who was behind his newspaper again. "We will need the car to go to church. More coffee, please."

Ma clanked the coffeepot onto the stove. "George! We are not going to church!"

BOB: You might need to stay home from church today, folks.

"See?" said Ma.

"Of course we will go," said Pop. "It's Sunday."

Ma shook her spatula at him. "We will be attacked by wild animals!"

"You worry too much, Athena," said Pop. "I'm sure by now that bear has been arrested." He tapped the newspaper with a finger. "Look here! A Fourth of July celebration at the zoo! Everyone is invited! We should go after church, *neh*?"

RAY: I sure do hope this doesn't put the kibosh on today's festivities at the zoo.

BOB: Golly, that'd be a shame, Ray. Nothing stops a party in its tracks like a half-ton polar bear on the loose.

Just then, the back door swung open and hit the wall with a bang. There was Ace, still in his pajamas. "Nick! Did ya hear?"

"I heard."

"Ace! *Kalimera*," said Pop.

"Close the door!" hollered Ma. "Wild animals!"

"Don't close the door," said Uncle Spiro. "Let's go!"

"Hang on," I hollered. I dashed to the pantry, grabbed some supplies that might come in handy, and headed toward the door.

"Don't forget," called Pop. "Be back by nine o'clock, *neh*?"

"Sure thing, Pop," I called over my shoulder as the three of us tumbled out the door. "Nine o'clock sharp."

Or never. Depending on Frosty's mood.

CHAPTER

43

"HOW ARE WE GONNA FIND HER?" I ASKED AS UNCLE Spiro steered the Nash out of the alley and into the early-morning quiet.

"Hear those sirens?" he said. "My money is on that spot."

So we slowed down and cranked all the windows open so we could home in on the sound of the wailing sirens.

As we got closer, the wailing stopped. But now we could see a squad car parked outside the zoo entrance, with its lights swirling and its headlights trained on one of the houses across the street.

There was Frosty, stopped halfway up the steps of the front porch, as if he was trying to remember where he'd put his house key.

And there was Penny, backed into a corner of the porch. Her newspaper sack was slung across her shoulder, and she held a rolled-up newspaper in each hand, like fat, stubby swords.

Frosty didn't seem to notice any of it. He stood in front of her on all fours, blocking her exit. He sniffed the air and swayed, like there was music playing that only he could hear.

Uncle Spiro pulled to the curb behind the squad car and turned off the engine. Now there was no sound except for the rustle of squirrels in the trees.

"What's wrong with Frosty?" said Ace from the back seat. "He's all . . . wobbly."

Ace was right. Frosty kept swaying, and he pawed the air once or twice, like he was trying to swim up the porch steps in slow motion.

And then I remembered. "He had his dental appointment last night!"

"Dental appointment?" said Uncle Spiro. "Frosty?"

"That's right!" said Ace. "To fill his cavities. Mr. Stankey said that the dentist could only come on the weekend and that Frosty would need sedation."

"Looks like the sedative hasn't quite worn off," said Uncle Spiro, squinting over at Frosty, who did look awfully woozy.

"Penny doesn't know that," I said. "What should we do?"

But before we could figure out what to do, Penny figured it out all by herself. She squinted at her target, wound herself up, and hurled a rolled-up newspaper.

That newspaper hit Frosty right on the nose. A perfect strike.

Frosty sat back on his hind legs. He looked around, like he was wondering what had happened to the music he'd been hearing, and then he toppled over and went to sleep, right there on the porch steps.

"Penny!" we all hollered.

She vaulted over the porch railing and ran for it. Ace opened the back door of the Nash, and she jumped in like a bank robber into a getaway car.

We were so busy hollering, and slapping her on the back, and laughing with relief, that it took a few seconds to notice someone standing at the car window.

It was a policeman. He bent over and peered into the back seat.

"Are you okay back there?" He squinted. "Hey—aren't you Bernie Lonergan's kid?"

Penny nodded, still trying to catch her breath. "I'm okay."

"Does your pop know what's going on here?" asked the officer.

Penny gulped. "He only knows I'm out on my paper route."

"Wait here," said the copper. "As soon as we deal with this here polar bear, I'll get him on the radio and he can come get you." He hurried off to his squad car, possibly to find the polar-bear-sized handcuffs.

"Are you really okay?" I asked Penny.

"I think so," she said. "Frosty is acting so weird. Like he's drunk or something."

"He had his cavities filled last night," said Ace. "We figure the sedative hasn't completely worn off yet."

"That explains it," said Penny. "Anyway, he never got very close to me. He just surprised me, that's all. I didn't expect to see a polar bear walking up the sidewalk at six o'clock in the morning." Even though she was acting brave—she *was* brave—I could tell she was shaken up.

"Sit tight," said Uncle Spiro. "Your pop will be here soon. And some zookeepers, I hope."

Over on the front porch, Frosty started to stir again.

"He's waking up!" somebody hollered.

I couldn't wait around for the zookeepers to show up. I needed to do something *now*. "Penny, wait here with Uncle Spiro until your pop comes. Ace, let's go." I opened the car door and hopped out.

"Where do you think you're going?" said Uncle Spiro. "He looks like his bones are made of rubber, but that's still a wild polar bear out there."

"I know," I said. "A black bear with white fur. We'll be okay."

Me and Ace crossed the street and stood in front of the house where Frosty was trying to wake up. No one really noticed us. One policeman was calling for backup on the police radio. The other one was hollering at the family who lived in the house to stay inside. I could see two kids in their pajamas, staring out an open window at the gigantic polar bear that was sprawled on their front steps. From behind them, the mom announced that she'd go see if there was any film in the camera.

While everyone else was busy, I tore open the bag of marshmallows I'd brought from home, and tossed one in Frosty's direction. It landed right under his nose.

"Bullseye," said Ace.

Frosty snorted. He lifted his head and blinked. He sniffed the marshmallow. He lapped it up with his black tongue. And then—I swear I'm not making this up—Frosty sighed with pleasure.

"Atta boy, Frosty," said Ace.

I tossed another marshmallow onto the front walk of the house. Frosty stumbled down the porch steps and snuffled it up.

That's when the police officers came stomping over. "What do you kids think you're doing?" hollered one of them. "Get out of there!"

"Hang on, Karl," said the other officer, reaching out to grab his arm. "I think I know what they're doing. And it's working!"

"But it's a *polar bear*, Joe!" said Officer Karl. "Shouldn't we wait for backup? Or a zookeeper with a tranquilizer gun?"

"Looks to me like that bear's already tranquilized," said Officer Joe. "Besides, you got any better ideas for wrangling this beast? These kids'll have it back home in bed by the time the paddy wagon gets here." He turned to me and Ace. "Okay, fellas, I got you covered. Keep going, but keep your distance!"

Me and Ace looked at each other. I wasn't sure how Officer Joe had us covered, and I wasn't sure I wanted to know, but all of a sudden I was glad that someone was keeping a close eye on Frosty.

I dropped another marshmallow, and another one, leaving a trail across the street, through the zoo entrance, past a still-quiet Monkey Island, and finally at Frosty's back door.

Which was propped open by a big stick.

"Ace!" I said, nudging him. "Look at that!"

But Ace said, "I'm not taking my eyes off that bear."

I opened the door wide and tossed the half-empty bag of marshmallows into Frosty's enclosure. Then me and Ace hid behind the big steel door and waited.

Here came Frosty up the path, followed close behind by Officer Joe. Frosty stumbled from one marshmallow to the next, slurping up each one, until he arrived at his back door. He staggered in, and I could've sworn he looked happy to be home.

"Stay back now!" hollered Officer Joe. He grabbed the heavy door and slammed it shut. Then he blew out his cheeks and wiped a hand across his forehead. "That is not something they teach you at the police academy," he said to himself. Then he turned to us and said, "Good job, fellas."

That's when two zookeepers finally came running up.

"What's going on here?" they hollered.

I stepped up and brushed my hands together. "We're just showin' Officer Joe here how to catch a polar bear."

CHAPTER

44

SOMEHOW, AFTER ALL THAT EXCITEMENT, ME AND Uncle Spiro actually managed to get home before nine o'clock, just like we'd promised Pop.

What was our reward? Uncle Spiro got a big, hot breakfast. I got a cold piece of toast and then got dragged to church.

How was I supposed to keep an eye on Happy? Luckily, Ace could go back to the zoo and act as lookout. Ever since last Christmas, when he barfed in the collection basket after one too many candy canes, Ace has been permanently excused from church.

"Hurry up, Nicky!" Pop called up the stairs, while I washed up and changed my clothes. A few minutes later I hustled downstairs, tucking in my shirt and slicking down my cowlick with a wet hand.

Ma stood in the kitchen doorway, still in her apron and slippers. Behind her, Uncle Spiro hummed a merry tune and helped himself to another cup of coffee.

"What I should tell the priest if he asks about you, Athena?" Pop said, taking his fedora from the closet.

"You tell him the truth!" said Ma, shaking a wooden spoon at Pop. "I am not going anywhere with wild animals out there!"

An hour later, there we sat, me and Pop, in a contest to see who could stay awake while the priest droned on and on and on and on. I had to admit: Without Ma there to give us an elbow at the right moments, we were both pretty hopeless.

I think Pop won the staying-awake contest. I'm not sure. I fell asleep. One minute I was dreaming about marshmallows and polar bears, and the next minute I was being jostled awake.

I opened my eyes and found myself staring into Pete's ugly mug.

"What's going on?" I said, shaking myself awake. "Is it over?"

"It's been over for about five minutes, knucklehead," said Pete. Sure enough, the pews were already mostly empty. Pop was nowhere in sight.

"What do you want?" I said.

"I got some news for you, if you're interested." He made sure no one else was listening, and then he slid into the pew next to me. "You know how you blabbed to Happy about Mr. Stankey threatening to shut down Sparky's cart?"

I gave a sick nod.

"And how Happy said he was biding his time?"

"I remember," I muttered.

"Well," said Pete, "time's up. Wanna know Happy's plan?"

Now I was wide awake. I didn't trust Pete, but I couldn't resist. "Let's hear it."

Pete glanced around again, and then he lowered his voice. "When Happy couldn't toss a cup of custard onto Monkey Island yesterday afternoon, he decided to wait until after closing time. He figured the zookeepers would find it first thing this morning, report it to Mr. Stankey, and that would be that. Sparky's would be shut down for good, just in time for the Fourth of July."

Holy smokes. Of course Happy would wait until the dead of night. And I'd walked right past Monkey Island earlier this morning. Why hadn't I paid closer attention?

Because I'd been paying attention to an escaped polar bear, that's why.

I stood up. "I gotta go."

Pete pushed me back down onto the pew. "Hold your horses. There's more."

"But—"

"Don't worry!" said Pete. "Happy never got a chance to toss that custard cup last night. The place was swarming with zookeepers and other fellas heading over to the polar bear den for some reason. And that's right next to Monkey Island, so Happy chickened out. Too many witnesses, he said."

All of a sudden, I knew that Pete was telling the truth. Frosty had had his dental appointment last night. Which meant that—unlike most nights, when the zoo goes to sleep without a whimper—the place had been bustling.

I gave Pete the stink-eye. "How do you know all this?"

He grinned. "I know stuff."

"Right," I said. "So, now what?"

He gave me a wink. "It's gonna happen in broad daylight. In front of everybody, live on the radio."

"Holy smokes," I said. "But what about witnesses?"

"Happy thinks he's got that figured out too. He wants *me* to do it."

"You can't do that!"

"Keep your voice down, you're still in church! Anyway, don't worry. I'm not gonna do it."

"You're not? Why not?"

Now Pete's smug smile faded. "Because I'm fed up with Happy, that's why. He's always hollering, and now that he fired Ace, I'm the only one left to holler at. If Happy wants a cup tossed onto Monkey Island, he can do it himself."

So, the bully was tired of being bullied. Ironic.

"Is that also why you threw away all the strawberry custard?"

He nodded. "Better than punching him in the nose, which is what I really wanted to do."

"Fair enough," I said. "But why are you telling me all this? You hate my guts."

Pete looked honestly surprised. "I don't hate you."

Now it was my turn to be surprised. "Then how come you've been beating me up since second grade?"

He thought about it. Finally he said, "I dunno. Habit, I guess. It's nothing personal."

I tried to let that sink in for a second. And then I decided it would take a lot longer than a second for that fact to sink in, so I just said, "Holy smokes."

CHAPTER

45

"ATHENA," SAID POP AS WE WALKED IN THE FRONT door after church, "today I will take you to the zoo for the Fourth of July party, *neh*? It will be nice."

"I'm not going to that zoo!" said Ma, who was still wearing her apron and slippers. "I'm not going anywhere. Nicky's little friend was almost eaten alive!"

"Penny's fine, Ma," I said. "And Frosty's back in his cage, safe and sound."

"See?" said Pop. "It's very hard to lose a polar bear."

Ma crossed her arms. "There is nothing you can say or do to make me go out that door. Especially, I am not going anywhere near that zoo!"

That got Uncle Spiro's attention. "But what about

the custard cart?" he said. "I'll need all the help I can get today!"

Pop settled into his chair with the Sunday paper. "You should not ask Athena to help at your cart, Spiro. I thought you found a boy to work for you."

Uncle Spiro and I looked at each other, and then we looked at Ma.

She rolled her eyes and said, "George. Don't you wonder why you've been eating only sandwiches for supper every night these past two weeks?"

Pop turned a page and shrugged. "I thought maybe it was too hot to cook."

She rolled her eyes again, and then she said to Spiro, "You will have to find someone else."

"But I don't want someone else!" said Uncle Spiro. "Please, Athena. Today's the biggest day of the year. You're the only one who'll be able to keep up with so many customers. Besides, they love you!"

Pop sat up straight and folded his newspaper. "Customers love her? Spiro, what are you talking about?"

Uncle Spiro looked at Ma, who shrugged her permission. So Spiro said, "You're busy down at the hat shop every day, George, so you might not have noticed. But Athena's been working the custard cart at the zoo. Every afternoon, for almost two weeks." And then a grin spread across his face. "It's a shame you can't see her. She's a natural. In fact, you want to know the real secret ingredient at Sparky's custard cart? It's Athena."

At that, Ma beamed as if she'd just been crowned Miss America.

But Pop didn't see it that way. "Athena?" he sputtered. "My wife . . . working? At the zoo? A . . . job?"

Ma tilted her head. "*Neh*, George. Your wife, she has a job."

Pop's face went pale. The newspaper slid onto the floor in a cascade of pages. He lifted his chin and said, "I don't provide enough for my family?"

Ma blinked at him. "Of course you provide!" She sat on the arm of his chair and laid a hand on his shoulder. "Remember when you first came from Greece? You had nothing. Only one small suitcase with string tied around it."

"I remember," he murmured.

"And now look what you have," said Ma with the sweep of an arm. "A beautiful home, a successful business, a nice car. A good life. We have all of this because of you."

At this, Pop relaxed, but only a little. "Then why you are going to work, Athena?" he said, still sounding hurt.

Uncle Spiro stepped in. "She's doing it for me, George. Other people fell through, and Athena offered to help when I really needed it."

Pop patted Ma's hand. "Athena, I am proud of you for helping Spiro when he was getting started. But now he is doing good business and can hire a nice, strong boy. Working outside the home, it's not fit for a wife. A mother." He reached down and scooped up the scattered newspaper from the rug. "No more."

"No more?" said Ma, removing her hand from Pop's shoulder.

"That's right," said Pop. "A woman's place is in the home." He shook out his newspaper and settled back in his chair, as if everything had been decided.

But Pop really should've known better.

"Well," said Ma. She stood up and folded her arms.

Uncle Spiro and I looked at each other, waiting for the other shoe to drop.

A few seconds later, here it came.

"Nicky," said Ma, still glaring at Pop, who was barricaded behind his newspaper, "go down the basement and find my snow boots and mittens."

"On the Fourth of July?"

She raised an eyebrow at me. "If I am going out there with all those wild animals, I will need extra protection." And she turned around and marched through the kitchen door, letting it swing shut behind her.

CHAPTER

46

T WAS AFTER ELEVEN O'CLOCK. IN LESS THAN AN hour, the Fourth of July festivities at the zoo would be officially underway.

Uncle Spiro headed to the shop to load up the Radio Flyer with custard and wheel it over to the zoo. Ma suited up in snow boots, trench coat, sunglasses, mittens, and her map-of-Greece scarf. Pop sat in his chair, grumbling.

And I took off for the zoo to find Ace. If Pete had been telling the truth this morning at church, Ace would have nothing to report.

But I still wasn't sure I trusted Pete.

When I got to the zoo, I was surprised to find Penny there.

"Are you okay?" I asked her. "After what happened this morning, I figured your folks wouldn't let you out of the house."

"They almost didn't," she said. "But I can't miss the Fourth of July!"

Who could blame her? The place was already humming. A van was parked outside the zoo entrance, and a couple of fellas were hauling radio equipment out onto the lawn next to Sparky's cart. In the distance, I could hear someone warming up on a bugle. The scent of roasted hot dogs was in the air. American flags snapped in the breeze, and bunting was draped everywhere. Whole families were already milling around, some of them still in their church clothes. And some fellas had even dug out their old military uniforms for the occasion. They looked proud to be showing them off, and happy to be wearing them in peacetime.

"Where's Ace?" I said.

Penny pointed toward Monkey Island. "He's lying in wait."

Sure enough, we found him in the bushes next to the Monkey Island fence holding a pair of binoculars and wearing an old army helmet covered with leaves and twigs. "No custard cups so far," he reported. "And no sign of Happy, either."

"Maybe Pete was telling the truth after all," I said.

"About what?"

So I filled them in. "Pete cornered me at church this morning. He told me that Happy was sneaking around here last night, looking for a chance to toss a custard cup onto Monkey Island. But there were too many people around."

"Pete's an informant?" said Penny. "For our side?"

I shrugged. "And now Happy wants Pete to toss the custard today. During the radio broadcast, in front of everyone! But Pete told me he's not gonna do it. He says he's tired of being bullied by Happy."

Ace snorted. "I don't believe a word of it."

I had to admit: Now that I'd said it out loud, I didn't believe it either.

Pete was right about one thing, though: Happy hadn't tossed a custard cup last night. But something didn't add up. Sure, there'd been lots of people around last night, which would've made it hard to go unnoticed. But at some point they'd all been inside Frosty's den, working on his teeth, giving Happy his perfect chance.

So why hadn't he taken it?

And then suddenly I knew why. Because last night, Happy had seen an even better chance to cause even bigger trouble. Much bigger.

And it all had to do with that stick.

I know what you're thinking: How could I possibly

forget about that very suspicious stick, especially after it had turned up in two very different, very suspicious places since yesterday?

But let me remind you that a whole bunch of other stuff had happened in the meantime, not the least of which was a run-in with a half-ton polar bear before I'd even had my breakfast.

In other words, I'd had a lot on my mind.

"Fellas!" I said. "There was a stick wedged in Frosty's door this morning!"

"Again?" said Penny, who hadn't seen it because she'd been ordered to wait in Uncle Spiro's car.

"Holy smokes, that's right!" said Ace. "I was so busy being followed up the sidewalk by a polar bear that I forgot all about that!"

(See what I mean about having a lot on your mind?)

I nodded. "And that stick had no bark on it."

"Just like the one that they found wedged in Frosty's door the first time," said Penny.

"Right! And yesterday afternoon I saw a stick without any bark right next to Happy's cart. I meant to tell you guys . . . but then we got into that big argument. . . ."

For a few seconds there was an embarrassed and guilty silence.

Then Penny said, "Nick, are you saying that Happy let Frosty out? Twice?"

"That's exactly what I'm saying! I suspected him the first time, and this time I'm positive!"

Ace gave a low whistle.

"Golly," said Penny. "Now what?"

"Now," I said, "I'm gonna tell Happy that he'd better not even try to toss a custard cup onto Monkey Island. Because if he does, we'll announce—live on the radio—that we know who helped a dangerous polar bear escape. Twice."

CHAPTER

47

THE PUBLIC-ADDRESS SYSTEM SQUEALED AND squawked, making every single person (and some of the monkeys) cover their ears until it settled down.

"LADIES AND GENTLEMEN! BOYS AND GIRLS! WELCOME TO OUR ANNUAL FOURTH OF JULY EXTRAVAGANZA! TO BEGIN OUR OFFICIAL CELEBRATION, THE RIVERWEST HIGH SCHOOL ORCHESTRA IS HERE AT THE BAND SHELL TO PLAY OUR NATIONAL ANTHEM. PLEASE STAND AT ATTENTION, AND GENTLEMEN, PLEASE REMOVE YOUR HATS."

And just like that, it was officially the Fourth of July. But could we enjoy it? No, we couldn't. Because instead of devouring hot dogs and watching the little kids lining up for the kazoo parade, we had to keep an eye on Happy and Pete, and be ready to cut them off at the pass.

We all took up our positions. Ace hunkered down again behind the bushes next to Monkey Island with his binoculars and army helmet. Penny wandered out to the sidewalk near Happy's cart to blend into the crowd and eavesdrop.

And I got roped into helping Ma at Sparky's cart.

"Nicky," she said, pulling me toward her with a clammy mitten. "We are selling custard like pancakes!"

"Hotcakes, Ma."

"That's what I said. Run down to the shop and get more, *neh*?"

"But, Ma! The radio broadcast will be starting soon! Besides, Uncle Spiro's doing the supply runs today, remember? Practically everyone in town is here at the zoo, so he decided to close up shop."

I didn't tell her that if we couldn't stop Happy, we wouldn't be selling any more custard at the zoo, ever again.

The fellas with the van were almost finished getting ready for the radio broadcast. They'd set out a table and a couple of chairs for Ray and Bob, right next to Sparky's cart. Now they were connecting two big microphones to a series of fat cables that snaked across the grass and out to the van. They propped a couple of speakers on the grass, and then they connected more cables to the public-address system, so everyone in the zoo could hear the broadcast.

And here came Ray and Bob.

"*Top* o' the morning, everyone!" called Ray to the crowd. They took their seats at the table and blew into their microphones to test them. Bob spotted Ma and waved. "Hello again, madam!" he said. "I see you're decked out in arctic gear today. A very clever tribute to our notorious polar bear!"

"Nicky," said Ma, fanning herself with a mitten. "What he's talking about?"

"He's just warming up his voice, Ma. Don't you feel hot?"

She gave me a funny look. "No," she said. "I feel safe."

There we were—Ace hunkered down in the bushes, Penny hovering within earshot of Happy's cart, and me at Sparky's cart, next to Ma. From here, I could see Happy's cart in one direction and Monkey Island in the other. Plus, I had a front-row seat for the radio broadcast.

That's when the loudspeakers squealed again. The broadcast was starting.

"This is it," I said to myself. "Let's see if Happy makes his move."

CHAPTER

48

RAY: *Top* o' the afternoon, everyone! It's your old pals Ray and Bob here, coming to you live from the city zoo! Wasn't that a stirring rendition of our national anthem, Bob?

BOB: It gave me chills, Ray. Happy Fourth of July, folks! We'll be here all afternoon, bringing the festivities straight into your living room.

RAY: That's right, Bob. And if you're here at the zoo, come on over and say hello. You'll find us right next to Sparky's Frozen Custard Cart, across the way from Monkey Island.

BOB: And be sure to say hello to Frosty, too! Maybe if you visit him, he won't try and visit *you*, ha ha.

Right about then, Happy and Pete started arguing. At least, that's what it looked like from where I stood. Penny hopped and waved, which meant that Happy must be giving Pete his marching orders.

I held my breath. Had Pete been telling the truth when he said he'd refuse to toss custard onto Monkey Island? Or was he blowing smoke so he could laugh at us?

RAY: How about that polar bear, Bob? That's the second time in a few weeks ol' Frosty has snuck out of his cage.

BOB: I don't want to tell Charley Stankey how to do his job, but I'd say he needs the name of a good locksmith, ha ha.

RAY: Nothing to worry about, folks. No one was hurt, and Frosty is back home where he belongs.

BOB: That's right, Ray. In fact, I can see him from here! Hiya, Frosty! He looks a little sleepy, Ray.

RAY: He had a very busy night, Bob.

I decided not to wait for Happy to make his move. It was time for me to make *my* move. I marched right over to the other cart, nudged Pete aside, and gave Happy the bad news: that we knew for a fact that he was the one who'd let Frosty out, twice.

"*And* we know that you sabotaged South Side Lenny's custard machine," I said, for good measure. "So don't try throwing any custard cups to get us shut down, or I'll tell everyone what you did, live on the radio!"

I had Happy backed into a corner. Caught red-handed. The evidence was stacked against him.

So what did Happy do?

He laughed in my face.

He actually bent over double, put his hands on his knees, and laughed so hard he had to wipe his eyes.

RAY: Speaking of Charley Stankey, here he comes right now. Come on over and say a few words to everyone, Charley!

Happy finally stopped laughing. He straightened up and glanced over toward the radio fellas, and then curled his lip at me.

"That's rich, kid! You have quite an imagination! Next thing you'll tell me is that the Mudpuppies will win the pennant this year. Pete!" he snarled, without taking his eyes off me. "You know what to do. And make sure Old Man Stankey sees you."

But Pete stood there, his hands balled into fists, and he shook his head. "Nope. Do your own dirty work."

Holy smokes.

Happy's eyes got wide, and he turned on Pete. "You'll do as I say. You work for me."

"Not anymore, I don't." Pete untied his apron and threw it onto the grass. His soda-jerk hat and clip-on bow tie were next. And then Pete was gone, blending into the Fourth of July crowd like smoke from an exploded firecracker.

Happy stood there, fuming.

"That does it," he growled. He reached into his freezer chest and pulled out a custard cup. Then he marched over toward the table where the radio fellas sat.

RAY: Folks, head zookeeper Charley Stankey is here with us now. You look a little frazzled, Charley. Busy day?

BOB: Hang on, Ray. Here comes a fella in a big apron and black bow tie, and he looks like he's on a mission. What's that printed on his apron?

RAY: It says . . . "Happy's Custard."

BOB: You don't say. He doesn't look very happy.

RAY: Wait a minute . . . Isn't that the fella who told us that whiskey joke last week?

BOB: Oh, right. Something about whiskey in Sparky's frozen custard, right?

RAY: That's the one, Bob. Now he's telling the joke to Charley Stankey. But Charley's not laughing.

BOB: A person should never joke about whiskey, Ray.

RAY: Anyway, Sparky's custard is definitely *not* made with whiskey. We know, because we asked.

BOB: You can't say we didn't try.

RAY: Say, Bob, do you see that? Now that Happy fella looks downright angry.

BOB: Charley Stankey doesn't look too happy, either. Hang on, folks. The fella with the apron has just pulled something out of his pocket. It looks like . . . a cup of custard! He's turning toward Monkey Island . . . He's— Uh-oh.

RAY: You won't believe this, folks. That fella in the apron is so mad that he's chucked a perfectly good cup of frozen custard over the fence into the Monkey Island moat. Which everyone knows is against the rules. Isn't that right, Mr. Stankey?

CHARLEY STANKEY: That's a ten-dollar fine, I'll have you know!

BOB: Whoa, Nellie! Would you get a load of that!

RAY: Folks, I wish you could see this. The cutest little monkey has jumped into the moat . . . and now he's swimming toward that cup of custard like he's been waiting for it all day.

BOB: And now that monkey has grabbed the cup of custard . . . he's taking a sniff . . . Now he's— Watch out!

RAY: Folks, if I hadn't seen it with my own eyes, I wouldn't have believed it. That cute little monkey chucked the cup of custard back over the fence and hit the fella with the apron in the back of the head.

BOB: Ouch! I'll bet that hurt.

RAY: I have a feeling that the only thing hurt was his pride, Bob.

BOB: I think we've all learned a valuable lesson here, Ray.

RAY: Do not feed the animals?

BOB: No. Never turn your back on a monkey.

CHAPTER

49

"**H**OLY SMOKES!" HOLLERED ACE, BUSTING OUT OF the bushes, his army helmet slipping sideways. "Did you see that? Maxene clobbered Happy!"

"She sure did!" said Penny, who'd pushed her way through the crowd to join us. "Atta girl, Maxene!"

I reached down and picked up the custard cup. Chocolate.

"Someone should've told Happy that Maxene doesn't like chocolate," I said.

We watched as Happy stomped red-faced back to his cart, while the crowd of bystanders applauded and whistled as if it had all been part of the planned entertainment. Mr. Stankey scurried after him, probably to collect his ten-dollar fine.

"Looks like Sparky's cart won't be shut down today," said Ace. "Let's celebrate with a hot dog. My ma gave me a dollar to spend."

"You guys go ahead," I said, because just then Uncle Spiro showed up with a fresh batch of custard in the Radio Flyer. And someone was with him: a huge fella in an army uniform.

So Penny and Ace headed over to the pavilion for a hot dog, while I stayed behind to give Uncle Spiro the news.

"Did you see it?" I said. "It was the best!"

He grinned. "We saw the whole thing. It was pretty swell, wasn't it, Sarge? Nick, you remember South Side Lenny."

Maybe it was his size, but even though the war had been over for a couple of years, the sight of South Side Lenny in uniform almost made me salute. But instead, I reached out my hand.

"Hiya, kid," said Lenny, pumping my hand. "It was swell, all right. Ol' Happy Harold finally got what was coming to him."

"That's not all!" I gushed. "We told Happy that we know he sabotaged your custard machine." I almost told them about Happy letting Frosty out too, but I stopped. I remembered Happy doubled over with laughter, as if the whole idea was completely ridiculous.

"What's that about my custard machine?" said Lenny, raising an eyebrow. "Sabotage, you say?"

All of a sudden, my face got hot. It was happening again: hearing certain words out loud suddenly made them sound unbelievable.

"Nick has a theory," Uncle Spiro offered. "He says that Happy took a hammer to your custard machine so he could get the zoo concession. Isn't that right, Nick?"

"Something like that," I muttered.

South Side Lenny busted out in a grin. "Well, son, I hate to break it to you, but it wasn't anything as sneaky as that. It seems that Billy—you remember Billy, Spiro. The kid you wanted to hire, but he sprained his ankle?"

"On the ice," said Uncle Spiro. "In June."

"That's the kid," said Sarge. "Well, it seems he was on duty that day. He was busy making eyes at a pretty girl, and Billy—being Billy—knocked into the machine and dented it accidentally. He fessed up the next day. Poor, clumsy kid."

"Hmm," said Uncle Spiro, rubbing his chin in fake contemplation. "Just like Eugene the repairman figured." He gave me a sideways smile, and then he reached over and ruffled my hair. I hate that.

"Well, I'm gonna get in line for custard," said Lenny. "I can't wait to taste that new flavor of yours. It's the talk of the town! You done good, Flapjack." He gave us a wink, and off he went, blending into the crowd.

Uncle Spiro put his hands in his pockets and looked me

up and down. "Sabotage," he said, and my face got hot all over again.

"Hellooooo!"

At the sound of that voice, Uncle Spiro and I froze in terror. I'm pretty sure that a whole bunch of monkeys ran to hide.

Uncle Spiro closed his eyes and sighed. "Hiya, Sophie. How are you."

"Just fine, thanks!" cooed Sophie Costas. She was still dressed in her Sunday best and resting that ridiculous parasol on her shoulder. "Isn't this just the sweetest little celebration? I hear there's a concert at the band shell later. And fireworks after dark." She sidled closer to Uncle Spiro and batted her eyelashes.

Uncle Spiro scuffed the dirt and said, "That's nice. Gee, Sophie, I gotta unload this custard before it all melts." He tried escaping, but Sophie said, "I'll go with you! I see you have someone new working at your cart. Isn't she . . . interesting. Did Athena find her?"

Uncle Spiro gave me a look, silently warning me not to admit that the new person was Ma in several layers of winter clothes. So I zipped my lip and stood back to watch.

And for all the things that happened next, I had the best seat in the house.

CHAPTER

50

"NICK!" CALLED ANOTHER VOICE BEHIND ME. BUT this time, it was not a scary voice. It was a Penny voice.

"Hiya, Penny," I said. "Where's Ace?"

"Getting another hot dog," she said. "Remember my sister, Josie?" Penny grabbed the hand of the girl next to her and beamed. You could tell they were sisters, because they were both tall and had a lot of hair. But Josie's was pinned back neatly under a little blue hat. She looked like a grown-up, refined version of Penny.

"Hello, Nick," said Josie with a smile. "Nice to see you again."

"You too," I told her, and then I said politely, "Sorry about your pinky finger on your pitching hand."

Josie lifted her arm and showed me her cast. "Thanks. My season's over, but it's nice to be home for the rest of the summer. Penny's showing me around the zoo! What do you recommend?"

I started to tell her about all the best things to see—the monkeys, of course. Frosty (if he wasn't still sleeping off his sedative). The elephant. Tank the rhino. But after a couple of animals, Josie became distracted and started looking over my shoulder at something else.

"Let's get some custard," she said.

Me and Penny both turned. There was Uncle Spiro, busy lifting the full freezer chest out of the Radio Flyer and onto the custard cart. Sophie Costas was still there too, gushing about how strong he was, but mostly getting in the way. Ma stood to the side, tapping her foot and giving Sophie the stink-eye over her sunglasses.

Uncle Spiro straightened up, brushed his hands together . . . and laid eyes on Josie.

First he went pale, and then he got all red. And then he smiled so big I thought his ears were gonna fall off.

I guess Sophie's smarter than I gave her credit for, because she took one look at the whole situation and figured it out pretty quick. She tried batting her eyelashes once more, but then she gave up. "I can get my custard somewhere else, you know," she said, sticking her nose in the air. And then she flounced off with her parasol bouncing on her shoulder.

Here came Ace, walking over from the pavilion. He looked a little scruffy, and (to be honest) so did the zoo. Empty hot dog wrappers blew in the breeze, splotches of cotton candy dotted the paths, and a section of bunting was torn and flapping loose on the Monkey Island fence.

"How're the hot dogs?" I asked him.

"The first three were delicious," he said. "After that it was all a blur."

"How many hot dogs did you eat, exactly?"

Ace gave a weak shrug. "How many hot dogs can you buy with a dollar?"

I did some quick arithmetic in my head. "Ten."

"I ate ten hot dogs?" said Ace. "They were worth every penny." He burped.

"That reminds me!" said Penny. "I have something for you, Ace." She pulled an envelope out of her back pocket. It clinked.

Ace took the envelope and weighed it in his hand. "What is it?"

Penny smiled. "Open it."

He tore it open and tipped a bunch of coins into his hand. "Wow! This is at least a dollar!"

"A dollar fifty," said Penny. "Remember the first time we went around collecting for the paper route? Those five customers who didn't pay us? Well, they all paid up, finally. And you delivered the papers that week, so I figure this money is yours."

"Gee, thanks, Penny!" said Ace. "How'd you manage that?"

Penny shrugged. "You owe Happy three dollars. And these customers owed you, so I wouldn't take no for an answer. Plus, I might have mentioned that my dad is a policeman." She gave a guilty grin.

"You're the best, Penny," said Ace, pocketing the envelope. "I'm going right over to give this to Happy."

"That's awfully nice of you," said Penny.

"He's not being nice," I said. "It's the only way he won't spend it."

But we forgot all about Happy, because who should we see in line at Sparky's cart?

"Pop!"

He smiled at me, but then he put a finger to his lips. Pretty soon, it was his turn to order.

"Next!" called Ma, busy arranging the contents of the freezer chest.

"Hello, madam," said Pop. "I would like to taste your old family recipe."

"Ten cents," said Ma, reaching in for a cup of Frosty Freeze. And then she looked up and said, "How do you know—"

Pop held out a dime, smiling.

"George!"

"Hello, Athena," he said. "Is that you hiding behind those sunglasses?"

"You know it's me, George."

He smiled and tipped his hat. "You are looking very nice today."

"Oh, George." And then she reached over and pinched him on the cheek.

CHAPTER 51

POP TREATED US TO CUSTARD (EVEN ACE, WHICH I should've known would be a bad idea), and then he strolled up toward the band shell to stake out a seat for the afternoon concert. So me and Ace and Penny squeezed onto a bench with our custard to watch the annual spectacle known as the Kidz Kazoo Parade.

Me and Ace had both participated when we were little. You'd think it'd be fun to be in a parade, but believe me when I tell you that it's a lot of work. You have to (a) stay in a straight line, (b) stay close to the kid in front of you but not too close, (c) toot the same patriotic tune as all the other kids in line, while (d) realizing with growing panic that your shoelaces are coming undone. Not to mention: My folks wouldn't spend the money for an actual kazoo once they discovered I could use wax paper and a comb, which were already sitting in a drawer somewhere at home. It's no big deal, except it takes two hands to toot a tune on wax paper and a comb, which really throws off your balance when you're six years old and trying not to trip over your own shoelaces.

BOB: Thanks, kids! Wasn't that a dandy rendition of "The Stars and Stripes Forever," Ray?

RAY: Is that what that tune was?

"STRAWBERRY CUSTARD! GET YOUR STRAWBERRY CUSTARD RIGHT HERE, FOLKS!"

This time it was not the loudspeakers, or the radio fellas. Somewhere, Happy Harold had found a megaphone.

"THAT'S RIGHT! OUR VERY OWN SPECIAL STRAW-BERRY CUSTARD IS NOW AVAILABLE! ONLY AT HAPPY'S CUSTARD CART, JUST OUTSIDE THE SOUTH ENTRANCE TO THE ZOO! COME AND GET YOURS WHILE SUPPLIES LAST!"

And then Happy made a big show of hoisting a crate up onto his cart and unveiling his supply of strawberry custard.

There were oohs and aahs from the crowd. The news

drifted through the zoo like gossip on the sidewalk after church. Pretty soon, everyone was talking about strawberry custard.

And then, you won't believe what happened next.

I mean, you *really* won't believe it.

But let me tell you: I was there, and I saw everything with my own eyes.

BOB: Strawberry custard? Say, isn't that the fella who—

RAY: Was beaned by a cup of custard thrown by a monkey an hour ago? Why yes, Bob, that's the fella. He's not easily discouraged, is he?

BOB: Ray? What's happening over there on Monkey Island? There seems to be some sort of commotion.

RAY: I suppose it's the usual monkey antics. Folks, don't forget about the band shell concert later—

BOB: Ray? Is that bunting supposed to be hanging down on the inside of the Monkey Island fence like that?

BOB: What's that? Sure enough, folks, there's a section of bunting that's come loose, and—oh dear. One little monkey seems to have taken notice. He's jumped into the water. . . .

Now he's swimming toward that bunting. . . . He's grabbed onto the bunting and . . . he's climbing up!

BOB: Watch out!

RAY: And now a whole lot of other monkeys have noticed. . . . They're jumping into the moat too. . . .

BOB: We have a breach! We have a breach!

RAY: It's true, folks! It's a monkey breakout! They're swarming over the fence. . . .

BOB: They're heading this way! Oh, no, wait. They're heading . . . toward the street?

RAY: It sure looks like it, Bob. There's a whole parade of monkeys making a beeline for—

BOB: For strawberry custard! Oh, jeepers! I can't look!

That's right. Dozens of monkeys swarmed over the fence, down the path, through the gates, and toward Happy's cart. Ladies screamed, kids pointed, and fellas held on to their hats. I couldn't tell for sure, but knowing how much she loves strawberry custard, I had a feeling Maxene was leading the charge. Monkeys swarmed the cart, and they swarmed Happy, and they even swarmed Sophie, who (for some reason) was hovering nearby with her parasol. They helped themselves to strawberry custard, and before you could say "hot dog," those monkeys had emptied the crate and disappeared into the trees.

CHAPTER

52

AND THAT'S HOW, ON THE AFTERNOON OF JULY 4, 1948, nearly two dozen monkeys spent a few carefree hours exploring the treetops and rooftops of the city.

In other words, it was mayhem.

"It's 1929 all over again!" hollered Ma. "I'm never coming back to this zoo!" She ripped off her mittens and her apron and made for the exit.

"Athena! Wait!" Uncle Spiro called after her. He scooped up the abandoned apron and sighed. "I suppose I'll have to hire someone else for the rest of the summer."

That's when Josie tapped him on the shoulder. "I've got nothing to do for the rest of the summer." She smiled.

Uncle Spiro's eyebrows shot up, and then he busted

into a grin, and something made me think he forgot all about Ma.

Just then, two zookeepers went running past with big nets on long poles.

A pack of kids chased after them, and cheered when one of them took a swipe at a passing monkey. They cheered even louder when he missed.

Some smart aleck in the crowd tooted siren noises on his kazoo.

A reporter showed up and started interviewing witnesses, and then a photographer showed up and started taking pictures.

Ray and Bob were laughing so hard they had to stop the broadcast.

A rousing rendition of "You're a Grand Old Flag" suddenly blared from the loudspeakers. The concert at the band shell was underway.

Pretty soon a police motorcycle rolled up and rumbled to a stop next to Happy's cart. The engine shut off, and a shiny leather boot reached down to flip the kickstand. The officer dismounted. Pulling off his black leather gloves, one finger at a time, he surveyed the damage.

"Hey!" said Penny, nudging us. "That's my dad!"

Penny's dad strolled over to Happy's cart and pulled his ticket book out of his leather jacket.

"Thank goodness you're here, Officer!" said Happy. His

apron was torn, his bow tie was hanging from the branch of a nearby tree, and his cart was a shambles. "Look what those animals did! What kind of zoo are these people running, anyway? I hope you throw the book at 'em!"

The officer nodded slowly and flipped his book open. "You the owner of this food vending cart?" He uncapped his pen.

"That's right," said Happy. "Just look at it! How am I supposed to sell custard here now?"

"The question is," said the officer calmly, "were you supposed to be selling custard here in the first place?"

"What are you talking about?" said Happy.

The officer held out a hand. "Vendor's license, please?"

"My what?"

"Vendor's license. I'm sure you're aware that in order to sell food on the sidewalk, you need to have a vendor's license from the city."

"But—but—but—" sputtered Happy. He looked around in desperation, and then he pointed. "What about Sparky's custard cart? Have you looked at *his* license?"

"I'm not interested in that custard cart, sir," said the officer as he scribbled in his ticket book. "You see, that cart is on zoo property and, as such, is under the jurisdiction of the zoo management."

"Zoo management?" said Happy, and then his eyes narrowed. "You mean Charley Stankey?"

"That's right," said the copper. "This cart, however, is under the jurisdiction of the city. Do you have a license or don't you?"

"I meant to get a license . . . ," Happy tried.

"In that case," said Penny's dad, "this is for you." And he ripped a page from his ticket book and slapped it into Happy's sweaty palm.

That's when Ace stepped up, held out the envelope Penny had given him, and said in a shaky voice, "Here ya go, Happy. That's half of the three bucks I owe you."

And then he bent over and barfed all over Happy's shoes.

CHAPTER

53

A S THE SUN WENT DOWN THAT NIGHT, IT SEEMED like the whole city was out on the lawns of the park, spreading their blankets and settling down to watch the fireworks.

Me and Penny staked out a spot at the top of a hill and waited for Ace, who'd stopped off at the bathrooms. We had a clear view of the band shell in one direction and the zoo in the other direction. With the help of a supply of frozen custard (not chocolate!) donated by Sparky's custard cart, Mr. Stankey and crew had finally rounded up the escaped monkeys and declared them all accounted for. But I kept an eye out on the treetops, just in case.

The rest of the animals were quiet, except for the

occasional roar of the lion. They'd all had a very long, very busy day.

I noticed Ma and Pop on a blanket a little ways down the hill. I had to give Ma credit for being brave enough to come back to the zoo after what had happened earlier. I guess even Ma can't resist the Fourth of July fireworks.

At the bottom of the hill, Uncle Spiro had spread out a blanket for Josie, and even though it was embarrassing and yucky, it was also, somehow, really nice.

Penny tapped me on the shoulder. "Guess who I saw at the pavilion earlier?" she said. "The newspaper supervisor. He heard about what happened this morning."

"How you bopped Frosty on the nose with a rolled-up newspaper?" I asked.

Penny nodded. "He said he didn't care if anyone complained about a girl delivering their paper. He said that anyone who's as brave as I was will always have a job, as far as he's concerned."

Good for Penny. She didn't have to worry about what she could and couldn't do, just because she was a girl.

"Hey, fellas!" called Ace, coming up the hill toward us. The color was back in his cheeks. "You'll never believe what just happened." He plopped down onto the grass next to us. "Pete gave me a buck fifty!"

"Pete?" I said. "*Gave* you a dollar and fifty cents?"

Ace nodded. "He comes up to me, out of the blue, and

he slaps the money into my palm and says, 'Now we're even,' and he walks off."

We all sat there, staring at the money in Ace's hand.

"What's he up to?" asked Penny, which was exactly what I was thinking.

"I don't know and I don't care," said Ace. "It's my lucky day. First, Penny gives me a buck fifty, and now Pete gives me another buck fifty. And now I can pay off the rest of my debt to Happy. As soon as he gets out of jail."

"He's not going to jail," said Penny. "He only has to pay a fine."

"Are you sure?" said Ace, sounding a little disappointed.

"I'm sure. He's right there. Look!" She pointed, and sure enough, there was sour ol' Happy, sitting on a patch of grass with—

"Is that . . . Sophie Costas?" I said.

Ace squinted in the direction Penny was pointing. "Pete's big sister? That's her! I'd know that parasol anywhere!"

"I think he's smiling," said Penny, shading her eyes from the setting sun. "I don't think I've ever seen Happy really smile before."

Neither had I. Holy smokes.

But seeing Sophie Costas made me think of someone else.

"I'll be right back," I said, and I went for a walk.

After a few minutes I found him, stomping through the grass with his hands in his pockets.

"Hey, Pete. Wait up!"

He turned to face me. "What do you want, pip-squeak?"

"You helped us out today," I said, catching up to him. "And you even quit Happy's cart because of it. I wanted to tell you thanks."

"I didn't do it for you punks," he said.

"And you gave Ace a buck fifty. How come?"

"None of your beeswax." He turned to walk away, but then he stopped. He turned back around and said, "I told Ace to dump all that strawberry custard last week. So . . . I'm half responsible for Happy's missing three dollars. I don't want that hanging over my head. I don't ever wanna see, or hear, or have to *think* about, Happy Harold ever again."

I nodded. "Fair enough."

"Plus, I want to ask your uncle for a job."

Holy smokes.

And then, all by itself, my mouth said, "That's real nice of you, Pete. Just for that, your secret's safe with me."

Pete narrowed his eyes at me. "What secret?"

Oops.

I gulped. "That you flunked a grade. But don't worry, I won't tell anyone."

"What makes you think that?"

I could've said, "Look at you, Pete. You're a head taller and thirty pounds heavier than me. Your voice cracks, and you're sprouting whiskers."

But all I said was, "Because until today, you were in charge of Happy's custard cart, and I know that a fella has to be fourteen to do that. But you're in the same grade as me, and I'm twelve."

Pete scowled. Out of instinct, his right hand balled into a fist, but then it relaxed.

"I didn't flunk a grade," he said, and then he lowered his voice. "I flunked two grades. And you'd better not tell anyone, or I'll punch your lights out."

Good ol' Pete.

54

I REJOINED ACE AND PENNY ON THE TOP OF OUR hill as dusk fell. The fireworks would start any minute now, so we settled onto the grass and waited.

"Do you suppose we'll ever find out for sure who let Frosty out?" said Penny.

"I dunno," I said, and I told them how Happy had laughed at me when I accused him of being the culprit. "It wasn't a guilty laugh either," I said. "It was a 'That's the most ridiculous thing I ever heard' kind of laugh."

"So it wasn't Happy after all," said Penny. "I suppose we never did find any real evidence of that. But if it wasn't Happy, who was it?"

"I think I know who," I said.

They both stared at me and waited for me to start talking.

So I told them. Because we'd all been through a lot together these past few weeks, and we were a team.

"Remember early this morning, when we rescued Penny from the polar bear?"

"How could we forget?" said Ace.

"I rescued myself, thank you very much," said Penny.

"I heard something jumping around in one of the trees. I thought it was a squirrel."

"Yeah?" said Ace. "What about it?"

"Now that I think about it, I bet it was Maxene."

"Maxene?" said Penny. "But the monkeys didn't escape until this afternoon."

I grinned. "I think Maxene's been getting out at night, all by herself. I think she's been leaving those sticks lying around. And I think she's the one who dug all that strawberry custard out of the trash and took it to Monkey Island during the night."

"Maxene does love strawberry custard," said Penny.

Ace nodded. "Mr. Stankey said that if monkeys like a certain food, they'll do whatever it takes to get their paws on it. But *how* did she get out?"

I shrugged. "Remember what my pop told us about that monkey escaping in 1929? No one ever figured out how."

Penny boosted herself up on her elbows. "So you're saying that Maxene let Frosty out?"

I thought again about all these animals here at the zoo.

They were safe. They were fed. But they were probably also really bored.

"I can't be sure," I said. "But yeah. I think it was Maxene all along."

Ace looked around at the trees that dotted the park. "Maybe she's out there somewhere right now."

"Nah," said Penny, lying back in the grass. "You heard Mr. Stankey. The monkeys have all been accounted for."

But I had a feeling that when it came to counting monkeys, "all accounted for" probably meant "close enough."

From somewhere in the distance, there was a faint sizzle and a pop.

"They're starting!" said Ace, and we all settled back, ready for the fireworks.

But then, out of the corner of my eye, I caught a slip of movement in the tree behind us. I squinted hard, trying to see in the gathering darkness.

Another sizzle. Another pop. And then . . .

BANG!

And up in the tree, briefly lit up by the fireworks, I caught a glimpse of a small figure, settled in the branches, calmly stripping the bark from a stick.

I put my hands behind my head. "This is turning out to be the best summer ever."

AUTHOR'S NOTE

In the predawn hours of April 11, 1921, a full-grown polar bear named Clown climbed over his eleven-foot-high fence at the Washington Park Zoo in Milwaukee, Wisconsin, and roamed residential neighborhoods for over an hour. According to the *Milwaukee Journal*, he knocked over backyard fences, spilled trash cans, and very nearly crossed paths with a milkman. No one was hurt, except—I'm very sorry to tell you—Clown.

Clown wasn't the only animal to escape the zoo during the Washington Park era (1892–1958). Monkeys broke out at least four times from the 1920s to the 1940s, according to newspaper reports. Monkeys that couldn't be enticed back to the zoo with ice cream or other treats were nabbed from treetops, rooftops—and once, from a girl's bedroom. In some instances, no one could figure out how the monkeys had gotten out.

Rules against feeding the zoo's animals were widely posted but were just as widely ignored. In fact, so many visitors tossed marshmallows to the animals that at least one bear developed cavities and needed fillings. The procedure was most likely performed after hours by a "people dentist," since veterinary dentists are rare creatures even today.

Frozen custard has been a Milwaukee favorite since the 1930s. It's made with egg yolks, and it's churned fresh every day. There are still so many frozen custard stands in Milwaukee that a person couldn't visit them all in one day. (I know. I've tried.) Most shops feature at least one special flavor in addition to the traditional vanilla and chocolate.

In the 1940s, delivering newspapers was one of the few jobs available to kids as young as twelve. Paperboys worked seven days a week, 365 days a year, and in all types of weather. Most paperboys were, well, boys.

Cinnamon and clove are two common ingredients in many Greek recipes, both sweet and savory. My grandmother, Athena Spirakis, always added a pinch of cinnamon to her spaghetti sauce. It was delicious.

ACKNOWLEDGMENTS

Many thanks to those who contributed their memories, expertise, and opinions, including:

* Mary Kazmierczak, Milwaukee County Zoo librarian.
* The Milwaukee Public Library's newspaper archive.
* John L. Scheels, DDS, wildlife dentist at the Milwaukee County Zoo.
* Gilles Frozen Custard in Milwaukee, for sharing their menu from the 1940s.
* Dori and Nick Chaconas (aka Mom and Dad).
* Ken Kozak and Roger Kozak, doting uncles and paperboys extraordinaire.
* Dio Deley, for her help with Greek vocabulary.

My gratitude to Karen Wojtyla, Nicole Fiorica, Tracey Adams, and school librarians everywhere, for being champions of books. And to Kelly, Tom, and Steven, for being the best team ever.